Trilogy Year

Trilogy Year, by Richard Segal, is a work of fiction.
Any references to real people, living or dead; and actual events, organizations or
locations, are intended purely to provide a sense of context or reference point.

All remaining names, characters, places, incidents, opinions and dialogue
are fictional, and their resemblance, if any, to real-life counterparts is entirely
coincidental and unintentional.

To order additional copies, please contact us.
BookSurge, LLC
www.booksurge.com
1-866-308-6235
orders@booksurge.com

RICHARD
SEGAL

TRILOGY
YEAR

2006

Trilogy Year

TABLE OF CONTENTS

To Tracey And Olivia

ONE STAGE BEFORE

"Sin's a good man's brother."
Mark Farner

It's pitch black in the morning on one of the longest days of the year. That alone must say something.

Jetlag writing is somewhere between happy obnoxious and punch-drunk, and the outcome is unpredictable, analogous to the 70th pitch of a veteran knuckleball thrower. Unpredictable, but with luck effortless and effective. Here goes.

I apologize in advance if the prose doesn't always flow the way it should. There have been unnecessary interruptions. Sometimes I get the feeling certain people were put on earth purely to annoy me.

For example, the "comedian" who fashioned an entire career out of unearthing the social condition known as "hat head" and announcing in-on-it truisms such as: "radio stations that tout a 'Top 500 of all time weekend;' shouldn't it be 'The Overplayed 500?'" (That's my truism, though.)

In my early 20s, I took a Greyhound bus to a rock concert. There was a compulsive jabberhead in Row 22, third from the last row of the bus and first in the smoking section (such as existed at the time), who lived to instigate loud attention-seeking, unnecessary conversation. Jabberhead informed an intense woman in Row 21 that smoking was not allowed in her row and asked would she please extinguish the cigarette? She gave him a death stare. Neither was successful.

I sat unobtrusively in Row 23, next to a quietly confident personality who insisted he'd done time with Johnny Tavares (talk about the hood, the bad and the ugly...), and I believed him. "Heaven Must Be Missing an Angel" had a whole new meaning after that. He offered me one of his two remaining beers. I declined, as it was too early to start drinking, 11:15 AM. At least it was then. He departed 20 minutes later to refresh his stock of tabloids and beer, and presumably tattoos. A couple of hours later at the end of the line, Jabberhead tried to make conversation with me. I gave him a death stare, and mine didn't work either. However, he soon stopped shopping his life story and I never saw him again, but indisputably he didn't adjust his behavior until someone did kill him. Laugh if you want. I'll be able to in a couple of years.

"Trite isn't right," I concluded this spring. I could only avert another folly by leaving the country, and quickly. My time on the edge was over, or so I thought.

It was 5:24 AM and the airport was packed.

At 5:41 AM, the bar was six deep.

Stag weekends have attained a new sophistication. Bert's Stag Weekend produces customized T-shirts; numbers on the front, nicknames on the back. Team player 6 is "El leg stag," number 8 is "The Olympian," and so on down the line. "Watch Out Malaga" golf shirts for the hens.

No prospect at the main bar, so I fan out to cafés with Tribeca-effect names and elevator music attitudes. Murphy's Stout at 5:50 AM? Let someone stop me. This is my folly I'm averting. A University College Dublin sweatshirt competes for attention of the Bulgarian-Turkish barman. Junior Year Abroad student is written across the forehead of her preemptive order of decaf latte, mispronounced, of course. Well, I'd serve her first if it was me behind the bar. A famous travel writer once lamented that he travels alone because he would not force his stubborn backpacker mentality on others. Likewise, I cannot think that many would stump up for a well-pre-dawn radio alarm for the privilege of being out-hustled at the bar by an eager, walking souvenir, knowing an unsettled weather forecast awaits. Nonetheless, unintentional humor unwittingly for my benefit, momentary outcroppings of beauty, unassuming historical relics, clean air, kitchen fusions of local ingredients available nowhere else... makes it all worthwhile...

...in cities where tall gothic apartments on bite-narrow streets vie for attention with football banners and urban clotheslines on balmy evenings, where an angry Dvorak statue stares down a citizenry as if scolding its paucity of classical musical education, where a baroque brewery walk trespasses upon abseilers scaling city cliffs for avalanche-prone stones, on beaches where the sun creates ripples of brightness on dimples of sand at low tide. Momentary but unforgettable. No, however, imagery that "evokes the Saigon of a more serene era." That I leave to the professionals.

"All Haley wanted was a family," confessed one biddie to another. "She didn't mind working, but she didn't want a career." Granddad, who can't get a word in edgewise, except to take granddaughter Shrek to the newsstand to buy sweets, looks like a cabinet minister and sounds like a coalminer's daughter. All things considered, I prefer Bert's crowd.

This is an easy airport to be on good behavior, even at 6:10 AM. Nothing to look at except the Norwegian mother and daughters. I'm sure they are Norwegian, except one of them is wearing a faintly reminiscent expression of a woman who loved sushi more than chocolate. There are many cities not to take a fiancé for a long weekend; they are not what or why you'd think.

Ah didah, I am also sure there will be no stag afternoons in Strasbourg. I'm glad to be leaving my coworker coterie of sore winners, shoulder chips and eccentric shoulder pads, mangled accents, if only for a day. The flatness of the Scandinavian English in the departure lounge thus arrives as a relief. The pronunciation in certain Benelux counties, however, irritates me. They substitute "let's say" for commas the way transplanted New Yorkers replace them with "ya know," and a loud Bridge Troll I once worked with defaults to the f-word.

My associates are as wedded to their rules and customs as nanny-statism is embedded in the national psyche, and I long to be free of this. What will it feel like to be free, and what has changed since my last trip to this part of the Alps, how many years ago, how long before the invention of universal email? I wasn't escaping then, I was experimenting. I was, to be sure, shocked that a small group of misfit personalities could melt into a coincidental breakout group during one long weekend and, aside from breaking the blood bank, create an entirely new and successful lexicon. But that was then...and long may it never return.

If I'm in luck, as I've been in other airports on the Continent, there will be a beer bar in the customs hall. How civilized. Moreover, my ironic amusement will be served if, in this city known for "Swiss-like efficiency," none of the public clocks will work. And glimpses of retired men sitting on plastic chairs in shaded squares if the weather is warm and dry, pretending to be taxi drivers waiting for a fare, or otherwise waiting for something to do or happen aside from lighting the next cigarette.

My first vision upon exiting the jet is a breathtaking view of the Alps, but my gait is broken and I knit my eyebrows as parka'd guffoons mutely stab the air to my left. No matter where I fly, trained ground crew will obstruct me from walking under the wing, inescapably reflecting the number of known instances that a wing has fallen off while resting, thus prematurely concatenating a business trip. The ensuing vision is of three members of the yobbocracy posing for a photo in front of the view. Radio Face 1, 2 and 3. It is North Yorkshire all over again. Primely placed inside the terminal is the obligatory bust of the city's favorite son. But who the hell did Christian Deppler bribe to get the airport parking lot named after him as well?

No less, Strasbourg has the Ringtone. Every industry needs a Crazy Frog, to act as a "New York cabbie gesture" to the snobbish establishment that necessarily inhabits each industry, just as each sustains a plagiaristic and fashionable DJ. And, aside from the smug Deppler family descendants, this city will undoubtedly be inhabited by refreshingly authentic locals.

The age of groups at Continental cafés is apparent by that which the waiter situates on tables at 10:15 AM. Young teenagers order ice cream, older teenagers beer, and grownups espresso and biscuits. As for me, my only requirements are a level chair, drinkable coffee, and a dry section of table for maps, journals, pens and aimless receipts. Yet it is surprising how often it is my luck to select the table one of whose legs has been gnawed short by an evil coffee house elf the night before. And does the service charge defray the labor cost of transporting my beverage 15 feet from the bar, or for wiping dry the inevitable spillage of the table's previous tenants?

Boy, can it rain here! Still, as I'm walking with an umbrella too large for any occasion except today's, it bothers me less than I expect. A young woman appears in the storm that powers down like horsemen in a black and white samurai movie. No, it can't be, because it isn't. "We've been emailing for so long that I forget what you look like," I mouth silently through the feeding frenzy of raindrops. "Phone tag, ear candy, what's the email equivalent? No, forget it. It will just make me want to see you, and Lord knows when I'll make it to your continent again. Well, I can't take you for granted. I never see you. Moreover, of what kind of relationship can our mutual love of blueberry almond daiquiris be the basis?"

In the midst of the neoclassical square, a makeshift grandstand appears, 21st century banners, advertising and TV communication links. Yes, it must be: "Beach volleyball was Here!" Surely not in this rain! Rain does *not* stop play? Well, that's Hollywood!

Automatically, I order the regional specialty. Automatically, it has to be good. "Here are your weapons, sir," the waiter says, wrapped in medieval costume and snickering like Smerdyakov, or Muttley. "Yes, I know. I have those exact steak knives at home. They are Brazilian. I bought them in Argentina some years ago." Crime of the century! Why didn't Gasputin tell me asparagus wrapped in bacon with sides of white radishes was on the menu? But who or what is Liptauer? I'd never guess so many kinds of smoked bacon were possible! I'm sure there's a corollary with Eskimos and their many synonyms for *snow* in there somewhere, but it's time to find a bar stool to fall off to recreate a moment of my last trip to the Alps. I smiled snidely to myself, like Mr. Jones' cat in the sour cream factory. I don't do that anymore.

As before, I must return prematurely to deal with, come to grips with, cope with (not necessarily in that order), the Externality, the Misunderstanding. The world has changed. 52 divided by 2851 equals 5.49 in their language, and indeed it is 11 minutes before 6:00 PM. It is several weeks later and I'm reeling at a standing-room pub in city central. The other partisans appear as if the product of a practical joke by their Designer, or if his hand slipped at the last moment. Hook ears here, a physically impossible haircut there. A screechingly-large propensity to spout platitudes and factoids. A wave of primary school teachers rolls in, eager to celebrate, drunkenly, the annual rite of passage by a pre-determined fraction to greener pastures and greater challenges. In this tavern, for sure no one will be ugly at 2:00 AM, and for sure none of them will be pretty at seven o'clock.

Oh, to be unwinding anew in Tampa, harmlessly astride Victim of Fashion Boulevard, or drinking anything but wheat beer at an under-maintained theme bar in Brussels, too ironic to be tacky and too stylish to be considered rundown. In a few days, I return to the scene of the original crime, no longer chasing anything, no longer running away from anything. The anniversary of The Inspiration. At the site, the precise coffee shop Café Crème, I will stare at the uninformed, expect another miracle and leave empty handed, disillusioned. Perhaps I'm the fool for presupposing miracles in the first place.

Still, it being D.C., there will be a lovable protest with innocent students, angry wannabe politicos, OTT-costumed urban ironics and uneducatable crazies. An illegal bonfire, in case one of the unsavories is anxious to taunt. A handful of bystanders, grinning: absorbing and loving the cyclone of democracy. Refreshingly, there will be no "girlfriending." However, as Martha Gelhorn once said, "It is only possible to fall in love with one war." The upcoming protests may well be poetic, but I'm a pragmatist and they're not gonna be my love in the time of cholera.

But that's not now either. I travel in the midst of unprecedented times, caught in the middle of the less-innocent maelstrom, benevolently suggesting a solution. An offer of goodwill is not an invitation to verbal abuse—and when I capitulate and ask for a favor! A definitive life event will give certain people perspective, yet others *carte necessaire* to devote themselves to the propagation of harebrained conspiracy theories. And others to air rage, my most immediate cause of stress. Anger management is not a cliché; it's a nation's greatest illness. Why did I turn deaf to hysterical commentaries about non-existent mistreatment by two passengers with name tags reading "The Clare Sisters?" This picture needs no caption. Sit down Sisters, the Law of Diminishing Returns is already accepted as fact. On the other hand, the intelligent science community may wish to present you as Exhibit #1.

Talk may be cheap, and words may be precious, but a day-to-day existence can be wearying. *One Stage Before* once carried a different title, but it stopped belonging. "Getting from A to B" is a common pursuit, and a well-worn string of words to the language lazy, but sometimes the only relation between the two is that both are uninspiring today.

Correspondingly…when I observe people in the street, I view them as character actors in a chapter or short film, having discarded in my mind those who are ordinary: The *Bay Street Journal* reporter who dressed for breakfast and could eat for Eden. The Anglo-Chinese woman with chunky beaded necklace, sinful glint, and non-descript boyfriend. The foolish tree hugger from my college days who called me "a person to know." I paraphrase to flatter her turn of phrase. These momentary urban heroes: nothing else in this journey is real, nothing is related. Well, almost nothing. Film at 11, pop quiz at the end of class, you know the drill, etc.

The academic brave enough to write the description: "an elegant mathematical proof," and who intentionally stresses the second syllable of words such as "runway," for effect. And who intermittently substitutes the phrase "by the way" for semi-colons, in dialogue. The man who renamed New Year's Eve: Amateur's Night. The coffee maid at Bergamo Airport who would wipe imaginary sweat from her brow and pose for no one and no reason in particular. The small-business squatter. The Einstein-haired passport checker at Bratislava International Airport. The Danish lounge singer who fiddles his guitar in basement taverns, wearing a T-shirt under unbuttoned regular jersey, performing late-70s standard bearers. The 26-year-old prodigy of a CFO for a fast-growing discount supermarket chain who looks like a young Bob Denver. With my friend's wit and comic timing, Denver would have survived *Gilligan's Island*. And skip to the end of the last paragraph if I've gone overboard on this topic, by the way.

I imagine a random stream of conscious inadvertently dubbed over a downloaded popular song, which on first listen appears to be an act of dynamic infiltration, but rapidly transitions into an exploit of brilliance. Sometimes when I'm focusing on these characters, I'm very quiet, but this poker face belies that I'm frantically envisioning future moves of these actors. And sometimes when I don't see anything interesting around me, I am also very quiet, but on these occasions I am truly bored, especially because I can't say out loud, "I'm being crucified to boredom and therefore I'm leaving this room."

It is not that people let me down that gets me down, but the how that is so unpredictable and unsettling. And it's not just acquaintances who let me down. For example, the worker who places paper towels smooth side down in the dispenser. When you refill paper towel dispensers for a living, it doesn't necessitate too much attention to detail to...an airplane wing just fell on the rest of my train of thought. Are weblogs "the new black," or the new "plastics," as Benjamin's neighbor tipstered him in

The Graduate? Or is the objective of a weblog to demonstrate how self-absorbed a person can be?

The View from State Route #135

The mature women were driving, windows ajar, in a coastal town, sensing the morning fog burning off as the piano solo on the radio intensified. As the sun appeared, the two simultaneously grasped their life's missteps. What they unwaveringly concluded was that "direction" in a modern world sense incorporated an omission to consider alternatives along the way. Did they simultaneously gain perspective and wish they'd tried the other path, or did they suddenly resolve to make amends for unexplained moments of ire?

Never underestimate the power of the fog burning off by noon. What they'd been searching for all these years was right in front of their eyes, and all I have to do is to read. "I cherish that you confide in me, even though what you confide is saddening," the driver remarks. "Still, it upsets me that you are sad." "Is that all it would take," we ask? As we now know what we wish we knew then, the answer is yes. The passenger, once angelic, is now merely magnetic. She whispered the secret of eternal happiness in her friend's ear, before laughing haughtily, sardonically. The driver readjusts her sunglasses to hide the tear escaping from her left eye, screeches a right turn onto Route 135, and resumes driving too fast for existing conditions.

Try as he might, the award-winning male author could not pull it off, a first-person-female narration. Women enjoyed the book, but felt the narrative was less than compelling. The men were taken in, and doesn't that about say it all?

The Lost Notebooks: only those who worked in New York in the late 1980s could have known the promise, or the premise, of the unassuming Americana shop or immigrant bakery where magic can come true. What was *I* so angry about then, during the Dangerous Days? I should have reveled in the Yankees' futility, when I had the opportunity. In retrospect, reviewing the lingering, lazy days on the water, spiked watermelon and static-free FM sojourns with no commercial interruptions indeed, this was the Golden Age. It doesn't take too many searches through the Mother Lode to relive that what we had was all we needed.

That's the good news, though. There is no middle ground and there are no sureties. Many times I've had to exercise my pocket veto when a colleague would "endeavor" to follow up. "Leave it with me," they said. "My answer I will never see," I replied silently to myself. "Follow up my ass."

"Thanks for taking my side in the debate," an innocent bystander said. "It's okay," I responded. "I used to work for the three blind mice (currently acting head of sales at the Bimm Corporation.) I can easily tell when he's lying: His lips are moving. Now everybody knows he's full of shit." To three blind mice, though, full-of-shitism is not a means to an end; as lack of lunar litter to a grand conspiracy theorist, it's a way of life.

So my Russian friend reminds me that the fish rots from the head, and in a land imbued with Medieval history, such a saying was fit for many a king. I counter: can a fish rot while it's still alive? Can you send the rotten part of a fish to Kangaroo Court? Do the three blind mice serve a useful purpose, to help me calibrate gradations of one-off misbehavior by normal people for example? Rather, I think it reminds me to act honorably the majority of the time, and to apologize earnestly when I don't.

Throughout this journey I call *Trilogy Year*, I have weaved two great secrets, three recurring themes, and three or four noble, terminal flaws. Well, what is it, three or four? Or is it three and a half? No! I'm sounding Seinfeldian! Take away my pen! Salt my tongue! On a more-or-less less ironic note, let me know if you decipher what they are. I welcome the feedback, as the cleaner stated, with due sincerity, to the white-gloved critic.

I'm bleeding dry of real world adventures and will shortly pull the rug from under this self-indulgent prologue. Moreover, I regret to admit there are tremendous ideas and concepts which ache to escape, as much as the dew beneath the ground during high, glorious summer, or bottles of High Life on elongated, scorching wind-blown days, but which are trapped by stress.

"There is both good and bad surreal," a longhair once said in a B-movie slacker epic. "Imagine if we were all entitled to one do-over, but this could only be triggered by the incantation of a beloved medley." The happy results of this release of stress *can* be experienced, he claimed, and I believe him.

One more point to clear and I'm home and dry. "We're gonna give you a little margarita before we start," the doctor said, and winked out of the corner of his mouth, after recommending I count down from ten slowly. An hour later, I was cured. A happy end to a long and miserable saga. "It's gonna get worse before it gets better," he warned, "and time will have to tell what happens after that."

ECHO BEACH

"It eluded us then, but no matter. Tomorrow we will run faster, stretch our arms farther."

F. Scott Fitzgerald, 1925

The Baker, the Broker and the Basketball Player

This story commences in 1937 with the image of a young student sitting politely in a third-grade classroom. The teacher instructs her eight-year-olds to sketch pictures of everyday people. With crayons and on artist-quality paper, she draws a baker and basketball player. Notwithstanding the economic and other circumstances clouding the times in which she lived, both characters smile broadly. The drawing of the baker was ordinary, except for the context, but the cartoon of the basketball player was aesthetically perfect, especially for an eight-year-old.

Mr. Trackelis is the neighborhood baker, a modest man and cornerstone of the community. In those days, cornerstone was more than a term of endearment. It meant he served as neighborhood mayor and ambassador, honest broker, and unofficial clearinghouse of information and favors. He generated mutual respect among his customers, and though not by intention, presumed his honorary duties exempted him from malicious acts by others.

Contract law exists to set boundaries between reasonable people, and to deter those who are not from crossing the boundary. Regrettably, it became necessary for Mr. Trackelis to take action against Randall Grape Loikod, his inefficient landlord, who offered little aside from a decent location. Almost predictably after the first couple of instances of won't-happen-again-ism, Loikod continually neglected his property maintenance responsibilities. Moreover, he failed to account for Mr. Trackelis' safety deposit.

Eventually, it became evident that Loikod's erratic manner stemmed from his association with Thomas H. Dakota, his domineering business partner, and addiction to games of chance. The maintenance failures reflected cash shortfalls at other properties the two co-managed, plus the removal of funds for personal uses, but there was ultimately a conscious decision by Dakota—co-guarantor of the lease—to refrain from spending his own funds on property maintenance. Enforcing landlord commitments through legal action was easier said than done. Dakota went so far as to claim that Mr. Trackelis had verbally agreed on a contract amendment which relinquished his obligations as co-guarantor. When Loikod declared bankruptcy, those motivations became clearer.

The neighborhood volunteered to compensate Mr. Trackelis for the lost services, but he was reluctant to accept this act of generosity (if it had been legal, the community would have organized a public stoning), because this might have provided legal absolution for Dakota, who gained many of Loikod's assets in the bankruptcy process. This was a seemingly minor dispute which spiraled, placing the good guy in the forced position of litigation. Eventually, a legal settlement was reached, whereby Dakota agreed to a reduced maintenance schedule and refunded a portion of the safety deposit.

When the little girl and other customers entered the bakeshop during the ordeal, he continued to smile and to deliver quality products—as if in defiance of his adversaries. Imagine how it felt to be an eight-year-old entering the bakery with her mother, recognizing on the one hand the baker's reassuring presence, sensing on the other the neighborhood's fussy admiration. By contrast, the inner turmoil of Mr. Trackelis was recognizable to almost no one. Certainly not to his two young sons, co-deputy mayors of the bakery, and only thinly to his wife.

We should not fully blame Randall Grape Loikod for the unnecessary incidents, for he was not ill-intentioned and he suffered many personal shortcomings. We can, however, only hope that Thomas H. Dakota understands how his behavior and actions affected others, and that he fully lives with these. Finally, where is the real estate broker in all of this, the man who pocketed a quick buck from Mr. Trackelis, then new in town, without warning him of the reputation issues that followed Loikod and Dakota? If a well-located piece of real estate had remained un-rented for months, perhaps there was a good reason. Being innately unsuspicious, he never thought to cross-check the broker for an explanation.

Considering the aggravation and sleepless nights, Mr. Trackelis would have been advised to underwrite the maintenance from the outset, thereby reducing the need to interact with Loikod and Dakota. Indeed, as soon as was practical, Mr. Trackelis moved to new premises, trading location for reduction in stress and aggravation.

The basketball player was a friend of the girl's older sister, practicing set shots in the school gymnasium. She gave little thought to the relationship between the player and her sister. She was only eight, after all. It is ironic how uniforms have come full circle since the 1930s. The smiling athlete wore pantaloons which ended somewhat below the knees. Moreover, the pace of the game is back to where it once was. However, long gone are the days when apple baskets were used to keep score.

Meanwhile, across the Atlantic, Prime Minister Chamberlain was busy enjoining the Italian government to mediate the growing political dispute between Britain and Germany. Italy would eventually agree in nominal form, much to the satisfaction of Chamberlain, amid words placed strategically in the mouth of President Roosevelt, and dismay of Chamberlain's first lord of the admiralty Alfred Duff Cooper, who would resign in a huff of disgust. The republic of Czechoslovakia was about to be dismantled. Closer to home, northern Massachusetts cities such as Merrimac were recovering from the worst floods in recorded history, with rivers measuring 12 ½ feet above normal. Another assignment of hers was to collect newsworthy-looking headlines from newspapers into a scrapbook.

Letters Home

Our story resumes a dozen years later, when we join the girl fully grown, and studying hard during her second year of college. Homework paused this Saturday, a New England autumn Saturday. The great American tradition of college football was in full swing, and this small southern New England college was no exception. The leaves were golden and preparing to descend to the ground, and the scent and bounty of the autumn harvest was the undercurrent of neighboring towns.

She was gathered outside the dorm with her circle of friends, gossiping about classes, professors, relatives, Hollywood and other scandals of the day. She and the others were unaware of the gathering gloom in Europe, which would soon again coalesce into cataclysm. That said, her extended family had been embroiled and divided by the battles-royal in Europe over the previous century. Her family had emigrated to the United States about thirty years before, and it had been less than ten years since they were able to feel settled. They were content to let the Europeans continue to fight among themselves. No doubt, the tragic and self-defeating internecine scuffles had an effect on her as a young girl, and no doubt she sensed the sigh of relief her parents and grandparents felt as they created a new and tranquil life for themselves in the United States. Her seniors had assimilated quickly, switching languages effortlessly. They and other economic immigrants became the New Americans.

After returning to her dorm, she opened the letters that had arrived during the week.

"My aunt is in Bermuda and she sends me swell stamps for my collection. I found a wooden door in the garage. Putting that on top of two boxes I now have a stage. I put a curtain up. My sister (who is called Mickey Mouse), my little three-year-old cousin, and I have a grand time playing show. Did you see *Love Finds Andy Hardy*? It was one of the funniest pictures I ever saw."

"Well, is there any news? As for us Brockton kids, all you hear about now is the prom. Most of the kids are so bashful about asking a girl, I fear some may remain home for the evening. Have your heard from your sister yet? You can tell by her *friendliness* and *personality* that she is from the House of Mirth."

"Tomorrow is Monday. Maybe I should say Black Monday because our reports are coming out that day. So far I just have my History mark and it is a B. I imagine you got an A+. Last Saturday I went to the movies. I know it, I should have gone to the game but it looked too much like rain. (I am a poet!)"

"Well I am mad now! I went bowling today and broke two of my best fingernails! Where are you going to college? A nice thing about Boston is it is near the South Shore. A nice thing about N.Y.C. is it is the World's Future Style Center."

"How's my darling sister? Don't mind my handwriting, because I'm trying to write backhand. The Junior bands are having a dance Monday night. Now if you were a sweet little sister you'd bring home something nice for me to wear. When the kids went to see *Macbeth* yesterday they saw Jeffrey there. One girl was going crazy."

"To my big sister, How is the most beautiful baby in all the world or should I say the gal from Holy Toledo? All the kids were glad it was a girl. We are now settling our bets. I went to the movies last night and saw *My Favorite Blonde* with Bob Hope. It was awfully funny. I am going to a fashion show tomorrow. I wrote quite a few cards last night. Told everybody about the baby. Will write soon."

We don't know for sure which letters were intended for her, which she wrote but never sent, or when they were written, because they were invariably addressed to the attention of a 1930s movie star, or a sobriquet, such as Wander Lily. They were, meanwhile, dated (for example) "Tuesday," as opposed to "Tuesday October 5th." However, those who wrote and received the letters could have had no idea that 70 years hence they would remain in pristine condition and would serve as an example of the fine penmanship, grammar and sense of humor that once existed among the young in our country, to say nothing of the historical significance.

Young and Feeling Guilty

Matthew and John Trackelis, six and three respectively at the time of the first anecdote, followed inevitably in their father's footsteps. Because the bakery was well established when John—that ever-international name John—was a teenager, his father decided to scrape together the money to send him to private school. In recognition of their own lack of education and the inherent constraints they believe resulted, Mr. and Mrs. Trackelis were determined to sustain the necessary financial sacrifice for their second son. Beforehand, though, they held a conference with Matthew, who was never likely to have the opportunity of educational choice. Matthew, being the less cerebral of the two, deferred to his parent's preference and his brother's advantage. He had recently completed high school with low honors and would be on his way to the fishing industry, a career of respect in Southern Massachusetts.

Poignantly, Matthew's approach to high school graduation was less eventful than his brother's. A muckraking journalist at the city newspaper (yes, even Southern Massachusetts had muckraking journalists in the 1930s and '40s) published an exposé about the admissions practices of New England's colleges, which purportedly gave priority to students from private schools, thus discriminating and setting in motion a vicious downward circle against public school students, who would never be able to catch up economically. The journalist cited John Trackelis as an example: the son of a business owner who shunned the local schools. As a child of privilege, he would be on a prepared path to riches, while ordinary students, and their children, would be condemned to lower-middle-class existence.

The journalist reached for the jugular by digging up John's birth registry, where he was formally named Ioannis. In those days, privacy laws to protect personal birthright information did not exist. According to the journalist, John and his parents hid his nationality so he'd appear Anglo-Saxon and thus more likely to be accepted at a private school. In reality, names such as John, James, Joseph, George and their equivalents, are so age-old that naming a child Ioannis and calling him John in daily life is sufficiently ordinary as to be insignificant. The damage was done, though. No high-quality college would risk inviting John for an interview, for fear of being tailed by the journalist. John was eventually accepted at a middle-of-the-road junior college, but, largely due to the trauma he suffered in the public eye at seventeen, failed to complete his studies.

Though it should have been the journalist who suffered guilt over deceptive and malevolent behavior, it was instead John and Mr. Trackelis. As if copied and pasted from a Greek tragedy, Matthew enjoyed by far the more successful career. Mr. Trackelis' sacrifice to provide opportunity to his second son backfired. To make matters worse, during his college studies John learned of the tremendous hardships faced by his grandparents during the Greek civil war, and the direct cause of mass migration to the United States. Those unmotivated or unable to emigrate were consigned to dismal lives.

Mercifully, as children Matthew, John and their friends were shielded from the trauma that had badly affected their grandparents' wellbeing. John was stunned to learn about his heritage, as it accumulated in his mind how simple and easy his life was compared with that of his elders. Therefore, he became even guiltier about his failure to follow through. The journalist, ironically, became a child of privilege himself, the toast of the liberal establishment, living large off the fat of wealthy benefactors and becoming an avidly sought-after commentator about social innovations, or an "instant expert" in today's language. He carried a free pass to rake muck with impunity.

The Jordan Marsh Years

Within a few years of graduating college, she was settled and married to a suitable man. It was a time of great rejoicing, for her older sister had recently given birth to her second child, a bouncing baby boy. As the couple looked toward the future, they concluded that to prosper in Southern Massachusetts in the late 1950s, they would have to combine their energies and concentrate on the regional hub. With a tidy amount of research as the backdrop, it became evident that Retail would provide the next wave of economic opportunity. Fortuitously, they could afford—both by temperament and parental support—to be patient until an appropriately sizable and versatile property came onto the market. The rest, as the cliché goes, is history.

As a working pair the couple was inseparable, but because they focused on different aspects of the business, they rarely strayed into each other's way. She would take time off to bear four children, but all things considered, combined family and business life quite seamlessly. Four was about the right number they reasoned, especially if it was two and two.

They had plenty of enthusiasm but little practical experience. Consequently, the pair relied heavily on fashion books and sheets prepared by fashion houses, advertising agencies and large department stores such as regional bellwether Jordan Marsh. They mimicked on a small scale Jordan's style and approach to business and customers, often wondering where they would be without Jordan's. They would send notes of appreciation to its directors, praising the store's extensiveness, beneficently acknowledging lack of industry savvy and recognizing that the store had little to gain by helping them along. In quiet moments, they would discuss the contribution that other earlier entrepreneurs had made to the nation's economic development. To be sure, though, all they lacked was experience. In time, they would become beacons of respect on a smaller stage.

Jordan Marsh was trend-setting for youngsters as well. Though the clothes and accessories in small-city specialty stores were identical, girls flocked for the chance to attend the Jordan Marsh Charm School, for fashion shows and workshops. The Marsha Jordan Club debuted in 1960, and the Club Card was a fixture in teenage purses. Its Back to School parties were true social events. Based on this success, the store designed a Jan Jordan program for younger teens and a Jody Jordan program for pre-teens. Membership entitled the girls to shiny black hatboxes, shampoo and toiletry samples from then-popular Breck and Tussies, and a complimentary visit to the Beauty Parlor. Its prestigious High School and Junior High Councils were desirable resume items. The councils were selected on the basis of crayon, paint and fabric sketches, along with a customary "Why I want to…" précis, in 100 words or less. In fact, many parents preferred the fascination daughters had for these clubs and councils to other distractions of the day.

Radio advertising was coming into its own, with mailshots designed to look like news bulletins. For example:

ADVERTISING
With conditions the way they are today, only the fittest shall survive. Advertising will help the survival.

Radio advertising, often used to back up other advertising avenues, is capturing a solid majority of retail advertisers, according to a recent poll.

Reasons given for advertising over the air waves were:
* To reach a particular market
* To reinforce the use of other media
* And because it's price is right

One reason for using radio is the customer is very busy without the time to sit down and read the paper, but (customers) do listen to radio while on the move. When using radio, be sure the person presenting it has an interesting voice.

Accordingly, they developed a healthy relationship with the manager of the local radio station. Though each of the children felt he or she had the requisite interesting voice, it did not come to mind that their voices might be half an octave or so too high for the listening audience. In any case, four-plus voices would have jumbled the message, so in the interest of family unity, professional voices were hired. Advertising rates on Boston radio were too expensive, though they did experiment with placements on the new independent TV station. But with unintentional humor not the objective, this project was quickly abandoned.

Store owners avidly awaited annual publication of *Copy Slants* by the Retail Reporting Bureau, containing tips from promotional experts, as well as secrets of legendary retail outlets such as Steiger's and The Hudson. Though seemingly predictable, *Copy Slants* was as entertaining as it was necessary. Within the action-packed, 120-page 1964 Guide were the following tag lines: "Pity the Poor Silkworm," "Meet the Fashionable Internationals," "Be Showered with Admiration in Pitter Patterns," "Come Fall for a Dress in a Soft-Spoken Red," "The Bright Beat of Summer in Delman's Summer Picture," and "For Tavern Hopping or Soda Popping."

And slightly longer recommendations for advertising pitches, with assorted typos:

PERSONALITY
The excitement is contagious. Daring capes cover lithe sheath skirts and turtle neck, long-sleeve sweaters…invading city, campus, country with the impact of an avalanche.

THE TOTAL LOOK IS "ON SET"
Top and legs match in snazzy stripes with a solid zing of

skirt in between! Cranberry, olive, sand and dark gray skirts. Coordinated stripes in top and socks.

DO YOU LIKE YOUR COFFEE BLACK?

Sue Brett makes it strong, sugars it with white blouses, collars and dotty black ties, edges it with black braid and cools it without sleeves.

THE HARLEY MAN ADDS A DASH OF SILK...

Only pure silk can reflect the classic character of the paisley print, now in ties of unequalled brilliance and clarity.

It was all happening.

By now, Matthew had given up his rod and reel and returned to his home town. Mr. Trackelis, though, had retired and moved to Greece, which was again a peaceful democracy. In contrast to his father, Matthew was able to evolve with the times and switch into higher-margin catering, reincorporating as Trackelis & Son out of respect. The father was homesick and uninterested in working out of a van. Moreover, he was tired of New England winters and of smiling on the outside. A small Greek village would be just the antidote he needed.

The Bickersmiths and the Haques

Living next door to our family were the Bickersmiths. Her husband had already coined his four-children rule by the time the Bickersmiths moved into town, but with their five offspring, the B's served up an example that proved the rule. The quarrels seemingly knew no bounds. It wasn't that the children fought with each other, and resented each other to the point of holding one another back, but every neighborhood issue became a point of contention: Frisbees that accidentally flew over the fence, decibel levels of the neighborhood dogs. It is better not to broach the story of the town meeting to discuss installation of new street lamps, to say nothing of monthly PTA meetings. Those tickets would not have sold like hotcakes on the day before Fat Tuesday.

As much as she wished the Bickersmiths voluntarily would relocate, or better yet didn't exist, instead of fighting back she instinctively rolled the bracelet on her left wrist and applied the doctrine of peaceful coexistence. She had realized over the years that fighting begets only more fighting, and dignifies no one. As a result, she chose to live with this steady irritant and ignore it whenever possible. Figuratively, she turned up the volume of something else whenever the "noise" level of the Bickersmiths rose above a critical threshold. The field of applied psychology was underdeveloped at the time. For her to have warded off the tension allied with living near the Bickersmiths, all she needed was to have known the proverb "it is better to be needed than loved," and manufactured a symbiotic dependency originating from next door.

In the days before political correctness, there was racism. In the days before racism, there was a vacuum. Across the street from the Bickersmiths were the Haques, a family of seven who emigrated from Pakistan during the early 1960s. As Mr. Haque left Pakistan to escape the ridiculous state that a series of inept rulers had left his country, he had little time for wearing a chip on his shoulder in Southern Massachusetts. This was, after all, a part of New England which had welcomed Newcomers for decades without comment. These were be-that-as-it-may people, and the Newcomers were free to make whatever kind of life they were able to.

Boston proper played host to a more sizeable number of nationalities over the decades, but also suffered for its reputation as a staging ground for political foment, and the 19th century journals published by Irish, French and German radicals no doubt propagated this reputation.

Color was blind in the neighborhood, and indeed honest behavior reigned in the Haque household, with the exception of second-youngest son Amer Qasim, or AQ. Invariably, AQ, for whatever his reasons, was inconsiderate and demanding. He acted as if he were AQ Haque, His Royal Highness, African prince of a 16th century fable in which all must bow to him and he had first refusal on every parking space. If he had been born later, he might have become the poster child for political correctness. Mr. Haque raised his family to believe they were Muslims, Pakistanis and Asians, and accented like many others who moved to the county over time. First and foremost, though, he selected this area because of its reputation for tolerance and normality. It was not family honor in the traditional Asian context that Mr. Haque advocated; rather, his precepts reflected a belief that living honorably was its own virtue.

Regrettably, AQ consciously instigated and provoked fights, and would later go off and do bad things—although fortunately, he was not strong-willed enough to commit serious crimes. Ironically, he chose to make his living in a field which required constant interaction with other humans, and he remained marginally civil enough to avoid being reprimanded for impertinence by his civil service superiors. Most of the time. The truly color blind would insist that AQ was from a different family.

The youngest son in the Haque household, Asif, was hotheaded at times, but calm when it mattered. Another young man in the town was in the habit of needling him, provocatively calling him "As If" instead of "Asif." Because his tormenter was widely disliked, many townsfolk hoped he would lose his temper at a more sensitive time. They wished Asif would exercise their frustrations on the troublemaker, but he declined. He wasn't needled because of his religion or skin color; remember, racism didn't exist in this town. He was simply unlucky to be frequently in the path of the troublemaker—who, 40 years later, could have become the poster child for road rage. At the same time, it is difficult to assess why the temperamental Asif was able to hold his temper when provoked. Perhaps that is just the way the cycles overlapped.

TV Landing

The 1960s featured *Lassie* and the *Ed Sullivan Show*, the grand *causes celebres* for the four children to gather silently in the living room. In one memorable episode, Lassie barks at a lone laborer operating a tractor in dangerous rockslide territory. "Don't worry," the laborer explained, "I know what I'm doing." Lassie barked, knowing full well that he didn't know what he was doing and what trouble lay ahead. She scampered away, sensing that if she waited for the accident to materialize, it would be too late. Moreover, she didn't want to be barking futilely on the hillside when the rockslide occurred. Sure enough, the rescue team arrived just in time to rescue the laborer. Lassie saved the day again. The moral of the story is not so much don't put yourself in harm's way, especially without a spotter, but rather don't say you know what you're doing if plainly you don't.

And Ed Sullivan was Ed Sullivan, even to those who disliked the program's wooden format. A little later that evening, her husband opened Joseph Wechsberg's book *The Merchant Banker* and read the immortal opening line: "I almost became a merchant banker myself." At that moment, his eyes diverted to the TV, where Agent 86 was about to deliver the even-more immortal line: "Sorry about that, Chief." He set the book on top of the 30-cent dividend check from the Commercial Solvents Corporation and laughed quietly through the rest of the show with the children.

This scene was a microcosm of a family that could do little wrong. The couple would parade into the store six mornings a week, she in her Dianne von Furstenburg dress and he in an understated plaid sports jacket. In the evenings and on weekends, they would smother their children with affection, conversation, and a sense of style. Without knowing it, she had become a version of Mr. Trackelis. Although he was confined to his counter during working hours, she was free to roam the full confines of her empire.

Her husband took care of the finances and other sharp-pencil business ends, while she ensured the fashions were cutting edge. She worked with the advertising agencies and was responsible for working the crowd. As she'd grown up daydreaming about fashion and absorbed the amenability of Mr. Trackelis relative to other business owners from an early age, she could not have been more suited to her role, or more content. When the children were old enough, they paraded to the store also, assisting the salespeople, wrapping gift boxes, lugging props, adjusting fixtures, moving inventory around. The family project was wildly successful for about fifteen years.

The Recession

Today, an employer would say to a know-it-all employee (who could both run his business better and simultaneously out-compete in an upstart), "Sorry, you've got a non-compete, you're stuffed." In the 1990s, an employer would say, "See ya, wouldn't want to be ya!" In the 1980s, an employer would say, "If you think you can do better, open your own store." But in the 1970s, and double-click here now to reveal other hidden clichés, the squeaky wheel got oiled. The family had owned and operated the store successfully since the beginning, and the talkative Mrs. Vivox bore features of the tractor driver in our Lassie sermon. Nonetheless, to buy worker harmony and experiment with empowerment, they offered Mrs. Vivox management authority of her department, autonomy to act in a wholesaling capacity, a generous raise and, ironically, just enough rope.

When the economy recovered in the early 1990s, it failed to bring Retail with it, and in many ways traditional retail never rediscovered the glory days of the 1960s. The beginning of the end was 1979, during the decade's second recession. For owner/proprietors, this recession was a full-blown body blow. A tentative recovery was underway during the Wall Street years of the 1980s, but soon-following banking and housing crises crunched hopes that traditional stores would regain their central place in a typical small city. Consumer preferences had migrated toward inexpensive, standardized, disposable products, or discount malls selling last-year's lines at the year before's prices. 'Fashion' and 'Style' diverged, the former becoming a misnomer.

Many mourned the death of Retail, and refused out of denial or introspection to move on, but she merely put away her Dianne von Furstenberg dress and got on with it. The couple quickly shifted gears and subdivided their building into small boutiques, operated by the type of enthusiastic, ambitious entrepreneurs they had once been. Instead of owner/proprietors, they became boutique incubators.

Reflecting their appreciation of loyalty, the family retained the pre-existing employees in as suitable a manner as could be afforded, or paid severance to those who wished to shift gears themselves, or retire. This offer was even extended to Mrs. Vivox, who naturally felt she was capable of putting the band back together, albeit on a small scale at first. Because the squeaky wheel still got oiled, she was offered the boutique space with the most prime location, and when Mrs. Vivox failed to meet her first half-year's rent or payroll, another amicable disengagement was agreed upon.

It was not until the mid-1990s that the family made peace with the Bickersmiths. Ironically enough, it was the Bickersmith's ropey dog Brutus who changed the tide. Brutus, like many other unsuspecting dogs, was in the habit of chewing all tennis balls within eyesight, and ignoring each and every Frisbee. On this particular day, Brutus haplessly and humorously attempted to extract a mildewed tennis ball from the chain link fence separating the two properties. She took pity on the frustrated pet and whacked her knuckle against the tennis ball, allowing it to break through and fall on the ground, to a glee that only Brutus could fully appreciate. She viewed Brutus as an anomaly in his household; why she finally decided to react is another tough call. Yet, the slimy ball was only a physical manifestation of what had been on Brutus' mind. His cries for help had been mute-buttoned for years. And years.

If we could have printed Brutus' sagest thoughts, they would have read, "You heed every screechy 'arf' of that prima donna Lassie, yet you ignore me, next door and in the flesh."

"That's some dog you have," was enough to break the ice. It had been some dog all along, but animosity had prevented her from admitting this before. At some point, though, a matriarch has to decide whether to swallow her pride and make peace with the neighbors, or live with the unstable equilibrium. Meanwhile, Mrs. Bickersmith had been too proud, uptight and self-impressed to break the ice herself. Throughout her life, the new matriarch had followed the path of least resistance, never stepping out on limbs which appeared brittle. After having sneered, lived with and overlooked, she decided to swallow.

A brief but pleasant conversation ensued, following which she returned to her house, smiling. "They can't be bad people, with an influence such as Brutus," she said to herself, "and they must have good taste to have selected such a puppy." In the event, the handshake didn't change the Bickersmiths, who would probably ignore the figurative peace pact before the ink was dry, having different recollections of the negotiation as well. Mrs. Bickersmith would revert to her maudlin outlook with attitude to match, and house too small for comfort. However, though unstated, she had also made peace with herself. The main irritant in her life, the simmering feud with the next-door neighbor, was resolved.

She went inside and opened a progressive magazine that'd been sitting on the coffee table for a few months. The feature article explained that Ben Johnson, Ivan Boesky and others were victims of a society that asked much and understood little of its fallen heroes. They should be forgiven, permitted to retain their championship medals and rewards, and invited back into the fold. She viewed this as a peculiar and contradictory stance for the magazine to take, in light of other subjects it had dissected in recent years. She became curious and suspicious: what is the comparative remuneration for freelance writing? Twenty-five cents per word if the article is independent, priceless if the article is financed by a special interest group? "They can go fuck themselves," she said to herself. "*And* throw away the key." It was the first time she would swear in perhaps 15 years, and possibly the last.

She then began to reflect on herself. She asked whether life passed by more quickly because she was fully occupied, whether her capped schedule caused her to miss something important. Were other obverses also true, she wondered? No, that reasoning would be sour grapes, she concluded. The past decades had been both action-packed and fulfilling.

Unnoticeably, she had surrounded herself with people whose company she enjoyed, and no doubt this added to her sense of joy and fulfillment. She had been both selfless and tireless, both driven and energetic. Moreover, others benefited from her retinue of activities. She was more than the sum of her parts. She looked at her husband and observed, "Look what I've become," smiling, because she quite liked what she had become.

She walked over to a cabinet and withdrew a box of black and white photos, to remind herself how the city had looked in its early post-industrialization era. Her husband nodded. "How quaint," they agreed.

Epilogue

The family's oldest daughter became a community activist in Upper Westchester County, volunteering to chair meetings of public interest at the town hall, agitating for quality of life facilities such as green spaces, playgrounds for children, and the aggressive pursuit of state funding. At the end of each day, she would sigh from exhaustion before giving her husband the thumbs-up sign one more time. The youngest daughter, always reading and ever driven, and neglecting her looks, studied law but side-stepped soon afterward to become a successful Wall Street financier. With a little more breadth, though, she'd have become the hero of one of our other stories. The oldest son, befitting his love of the outdoors, became a forester, vet and weekend guide.

After the fall of the Berlin Wall, the youngest son abruptly sold his stake in his medical practice to travel to Eastern Europe. He was mesmerized as the graffiti-laden Wall was dismantled live on CNN and felt robbed that he had not been there at the time, witnessing history and soaking in the energy.

He knew he must travel immediately; this was a snapshot of history, and soon the countries would never be the same. His plan was uncomplicated: fly to Bucharest and traverse the region northwest until he reached Estonia. His first inclination was to drive, but he feared being shut down at borders by independent-minded customs police. Luckily for him, as bad as the trains were, the roads were worse. Perhaps altruistically, perhaps naively, he offered medical services wherever he stopped and stayed, wherever there was a critical mass of English spoken. It was partly his idea as well to raise spending money in this manner, but upon discovering the pittance that highly qualified doctors received in Eastern Europe, he reverted to volunteering his expertise part-time in public clinics, and acting as goodwill ambassador to European and American aid agencies the rest.

One of his parents' lessees thoughtfully gave him a travel journal, which he promised to fill with notes and recollections. Riding on slow trains, his capacity for note-taking was ample. He was impressed both by the enthusiasm and resignation that he witnessed: some were ever hopeful that a new dawn was upon them; others were completely broken. He felt betrayed by the party lines spewed by his own government: though corrupt rulers and business interests had become deeply ingrained, and the environment polluted beyond belief, the Soviet Union was no evil empire. It was a flimsy house of cards held together by propaganda from each side. Despite misinformation about low standards of living, TVs, video players and other home appliances were commonplace, and traffic jams were as begrudgingly accepted as at home. The policy of isolating the Eastern bloc, enemy-fying its citizens, and enforcing an information blackout had been an utter crock. To a Russian as much as to an American, good time rock & roll was good time rock & roll.

The food was plentiful and at times fascinating and delicious, but without variation. Meals were all in the home, with hardly any restaurants open to the non-elite. Food-wise, he always looked forward to the next country, to be surprised and intrigued by the national dish, but also he ached for variation. The food was recognizable yet so different; spiced beef, white fish, rye bread, berries. He loved the proverbs, born of depression and repression, that survived the Wall: the bear stepped on your ear, one fisherman sees another from afar, all cats are gray at night, a fly will not get into a closed mouth, etc.

He daydreamed of discovering long-lost relatives in villages where they would speak passable English. He'd break bread with distant cousins, drink toasts and hold audiences with village elders. He mentally conjured meeting a too-good-to-be-true young woman in the final country on his route—they'd marry, he'd stay and work the land. In winter time, he'd teach their children to make snow angels.

He grasped three seminal paperbacks left on a seat by a traveling American. Having been away for some time, he'd never heard of them. *The High School Review*, a rock opera; *Accident Week*, a parody of early reality TV; and *Sparks From Krakatoa*, an angry indictment of realpolitik. He pictured the performers of *High School Review* practicing the so-called Victory Walk up and down aisles of the train, singing "White Dopes on Punk" and "Recess Appointment." He imagined the legendary reporter Graham Jay pestering a Kazakh apparatchik about an unreported explosion, a Peruvian dictator about a preventable train crash. He read the first few chapters of each, before returning them to their original resting place. Crazy, yet beautiful. On another seat were liner notes to the

CD: "A Song for April." He gulped an unaccustomed breath of nostalgia for springtime in New England.

Why do paperbacks travel in threes? he wondered, and visualized sets of paperbacks he had read. He mentally scanned images from his journey: baroque clock towers, second-hand trolleys inching through town, grandmothers directing children, eager college students scampering into buildings, bank tellers nervously trying out their English, housewives proudly examining passport photos. How relieved the young people seemed that Communism was over.

He then contemplated the grayer side of the Transition, and frowned: translations of editorials from the liberal press, conversations overheard, body language from the matron of Bread Store 126, a municipality's singular privatization success story. He gave no consideration to the possibility that the Wall was less spontaneous than appeared on TV or that many of the Communist rulers had laid a trap for their democratic successors to fall into. While the falls of government were nearly concurrent, leading to simultaneous rejoicing among the populace, successor governments ranged from vibrant to unreconstructed. The true revolutions did not transpire until the following decade. Moreover, as with his imaginary field in the final country on his route, durable recovery of a long-barren economy can not arise without hard work.

He eventually returned to the United States with his Austrian wife and settled in New York. They arrived in May 2000, just in time for his parents' retirement party. After a few months' search, he accepted a role as medical advisor for the International Rescue Committee, not recognizing the irony. His notes, as yet, remain to be transcribed.

I will not pretend this story concludes with the good guys holding hands in a Friendship Circle: the family, the Khans, the Trackelises, the unnamed basketball player and Brutus. I will say, though, and any fairytale-ologist will affirm: this being fiction, as much as possible all lived happily ever after. And that is as good a unifying theme as any.

THE SPIN DOCTORS

"You could be king, if she believed your story."
Cashman/West

Swish, Swish

I claimed to be the poster child for voter apathy, but she had other ideas on her mind. It was the start of the "most important election of our time," and divisive polarization was running high. So when I allowed myself to be lured into a skin-deep petition drive by a twenty-something in a DNC T-shirt, I knew a tongue-lashing awaited. For when you reciprocate eye contact with a campaign volunteer, but fail to associate her right-thinking selflessness with the 21st century equivalent of "right on, sister," that pegs you as a Republican.

Two business colleagues and I were sitting at an outdoor café in this far-from-one-Starbucks town. Across the street was evidence that in one American city, at least, there was an era in which baroque grandiosity was king. It was an enviable day, with the temperature halfway between "any warmer and you'd start sweating" and "any colder and you'd see your breath in the air." In enjoying the cloudless sunshine between conference sessions, I was taking a rain check on a side-trip to Monchos Music, a well-known emporium of swing, jazz and folk rock. I greatly enjoyed browsing the secondhand shops of America's seven-figure metropolis for musical hidden gems.

"So what about your contribution?" she appealed, after losing patience with my multitasking. "We can really use the cashish."

I edited the topic. "Okay, I confess. I pretended not to notice you campaigners for so long because it took me 20 minutes to decide how to break the ice—to think up the line, 'Sorry, but I'm the poster child for political apathy.'"

"Oh, that's cute," she replied, and tried to look alluring in an SJP-in-*Vogue* kind of way, which obviously was incongruous, before posing her same question with a facial expression.

"Don't think so. There's no way I'm funding the DNC. I may agree with your chatter about the Candidate, but I don't see why the Committee's plowing all its money into a race it can't win, when what my country needs is legislative balance, which means more self-introspection and more resources to the congressional races. If, with the sloppy economy that we suffer and the oafish protectionism your Opponent practices, you lose ground in the House and Senate, that's a translucent product of a wretched strategy. Second, the transparency of the DNC speaks for itself. But third, and most important, I know what DNC stands for: Do Not Contribute."

"What?!" she screamed. "I can't believe how much of my valuable time you've wasted. You can't do that. You can't just screw around with someone asking for money without giving it to them afterwards."

My colleagues and I looked at each other in amazement, biting our lips to repress the guffaws. This was too much for Jeff. "Did hear yourself? If either of us had said that, we'd be booted into political correctness jail..."

A meek apology followed. "I didn't mean it that way."

"Listen, *I'm* not going to contribute," I explained. "But my two colleagues here, they're card-carrying. I'm sure they'll be happy to donate. What about you, Jeff?"

"Forgive me," Jeff excused in his broad Cleveland accent, "my wife already gave at home."

"Oh. Jimmie?" I volleyed.

Jimmie paused for a moment. "Yeah, I'll sign up. What's the ante?"

She paused. "Fifty dollahs is..."

Jimmie interrupts. "Consider it done. Do you take checks or do you want my credit card?" He scans the sheet, which gives the impression more of a magazine insert than a national political action committee campaign drive pro forma. He examines the fine print and squints a few times before noticing a line for credit card information. He pulls out his wallet, extracts a card and copies the digits. Jeff and I watch in silence, until she breaks it.

"So, what are you guys doing in D.C.?"

"We're here for a conference on municipal finance. Most of the time, we travel the country selling bond advice," Jeff replied.

"Did you say you go around the country selling bongs?"

Given our attire, especially Jimmy with his tidy trompe-de-Bloomingdale's styling, I thought she had misheard "bonds" for "bombs," not "bongs."

We giggled. "No, bonds," I corrected. "Municipal bonds. We don't actually sell them. We provide advice to city governments that need to raise money for civil engineering projects, pre-fund pension requirements, advance revenue bonds. Things like that. Ordinarily, cities have their own staff make these decisions, or allow their investment banks to make the decisions for them. But the first is penny wise, pound foolish and the second is riddled with conflicts. We only provide advice, but if the municipality is above half a mill in population, it's cost-effective."

"Oh," she sighed, "I liked it better when I thought you were dressed in suits to sell *bongs*."

Jimmy finishes, scans his handwriting, and delivers the signed sheet to our new acquaintance.

A pleased look appears on her face, and she is re-energized to go on the attack. But whatever she said, I wasn't paying attention.

"No," I corrected, "I *am* not donating, I *am* not a Republican, and I *will* vote for whoever I feel like...whenever I decide. Furthermore, you should *thank me*, for it is I who raised fifty dollars for your cause. In addition, I know you're going to steal my slogan. When those you pester look past you, you're going to pester again: 'Don't be a poster child for political apathy!' In fact, four years from now, when the three of us are back for the 14th annual municipal finance conference, you'll be volunteering on this same street. You won't recognize my face and will say to me, 'Don't be the poster child for political apathy. Donate TODAY!'"

She half-giggled, half-grizzled. Women like her were not my Kryptonite.

She said thanks to Jimmy, avoided eye contact with Jeff, and reluctantly thanked me for the assist, before running off and unwittingly belly-butting her fellow volunteers.

I was relatively confident that she was out of earshot when I exhaled rhetorically, "If they're trying to raise money, they should have one person who knows how to sell, rather than six who are useless..."

Jimmy nodded courteously. "You had to prospect for her, *and* close the deal."

"She had no sales ability," I agreed. "Unlike you, who could sell rain to the Flemish, or Haagen-Dazs to the Danes..."

Jeff's frustration boiled over again and he quailed, "Or another hole in the head to my ex-boss. Why does the DNC unleash those DiNKs?!?"

I was taken aback by his use of a phrase I understood to be vulgar. "Huh!? DiNKs?"

"Do Nothing, Know-it-alls," he explained.

"Because they're cheap," Jimmy affirmed, "and the purpose of letting them out on the street is to raise visibility, rather than money." He evidently thought she was more attractive than I did.

"Very cheap," I acknowledged to Jeff. "I was thinking Annoying Know-it-Alls, but I like your phrase better." Despite the excellent, though unplanned, one-liners, she was very annoying. "And since I have you on my side, about those volunteers," I tested, "I'm sure I heard them discuss their reservation for Chinese 'Shabu Shabu.' I may be uncultured, but at least I know that 'Shabu Shabu' means 'Swish Swish' in Japanese. They will grow up to be Sushi Socialists like their mothers."

But Jeff went from irritated to testy. "Maybe you felt hassled because you really are the closet Republican that she accused—"

"No," I rebutted. "I may be stressed by politics, very stressed, but I'm not a closet Republican."

They'd never have guessed the cause of my stress. I was in fact a dangerous political operative, whose activities were indeed subversive to the cozy duopoly of national political parties and their entrenched special interests. But we're getting to that later.

And thus I changed the subject with a pretend laugh. "I knew she'd be thrown by the phrase 'muni bonds,' but that particular word association I did not suspect," I offered.

"That was a walk-off home run reaction all right," Jimmy claimed.

"Barry U.S. Bonds." More word association from Jeff.

"Steroids," I thought to myself. "Well guys," I said, "the only way your Candidate is going to win is if he uses performance-enhancing drugs with masking agents on the campaign trail, because the Democratic Party machine is dysfunctional. Fortunately, I have no party allegiance and will uncompromisingly exercise this voting freedom on Election Day."

They ambivalently nodded, wearing strained looks which plainly wrote hopes that fury over "the smirk" would tip the scales come November.

"Nonetheless, I do deserve points for service to mankind for my performance..." I lobbed.

"Hmmm?" they echoed, in unison.

"Yeah, of course, for nobly chatting up the ugh...," I boasted.

"Ah, that reminds me," Jimmy interrupted, in a way that reinforced our impression he found the girl appealing. "A question I forgot to ask you the other day. Is Patricia a common name in Germany?"

I looked at him blankly.

"Her last name sounded German..." he said.

"Oh, yeah," I recalled suddenly, shaking my head slightly. "International birth names were very popular in Switzerland 30 years ago."

"She asked if you wouldn't mind returning her phone call," he said.

"Yeah, I need to do that. If she calls again, could you transfer it to my cell phone?" I asked.

"Sorry," he declined, "that's between you and her."

The Client Meeting

We were in Northern California to meet with the medium-sized city known as Ruritania. We had dispensed with the pleasantries and each had our cup of coffee, bottle of water, Cokes, or whatever-you-got. I was along as technical advisor with the Big Two, Jimmy and Jeff. It was my job to present our quantitative analysis and modeling procedures, and to wear horn-rimmed glasses if Jimmy felt I'd look like more of a bookworm that way. Well, he was the account manager.

We had breezed through the PowerPoint presentation and Jeff was explaining competitive advantage and demarcation relative to our competitors. Jimmy felt the meeting beginning to drift, and decided to seize the momentum.

"Excuse me, Jeff, if I could interrupt for a moment," he cut in with max politeness, but which prompted Jeff to bristle silently regardless. "Mr. Smythe, if I may, I should boil this down into what your options are. First, you can choose us. I'll come back to that at the end.

"Second, you could continue along the same road, which is to accept the recommendation of the low-bid investment bank, but you will be left with an underwriting at a particular point on a line, without knowing whether you are at the right point on the line. You don't know what their fee structure is. They maintain you are not liable for any cash outlays outright, but is it not clear they're building their cost base into the structure? Imagine their overhead costs alone, in the event you hire them. And, they have to add part of the overhead costs for their failed pitches. Our overheads are lower, partly because we have fewer staff, but also because we don't spend any time spinning our wheels. Finally, for all you know, they could be colluding with other investment banks, to drive up issuance costs for all municipalities.

"Third, you could choose another pure consulting firm, one which charges a lower fee than we do. To do that, it must either staff less-experienced advisors—has-beens and never-weres, ha ha said the clown—or submit an invoice also to the investment bank they recommend you work with, in which case their independence is suspect.

"So, you could select us. We charge, for the services we provide, the equivalent of a middle-ranking bureaucrat's salary. Now, we're all capable in municipal finance. I'll grant us and most of the comp that. However, our firm is independent by design, devoid of conflict of interest. We have no affiliation with an investment bank, formal or informal. Once we outline your financing options, we advocate that you auction this opportunity to the most competitive underwriter. Call it ruthless, but this is your taxpayer's money we're talkin' about, not theirs.

"Ordinarily, when we travel the length of the country and deliver a customized presentation, we give it the hard sell. However, I can sense that we shouldn't rush you. What I suggest you do instead is take one of the other routes I outlined. We're working with another new customer this quarter, the city of Fredovnic. Compare your results and after-sale satisfaction with his, look at relative budget numbers and, if you want, call us again in three to six months."

Jimmy opened his PDA, wrote down contact details of the finance director of Fredovnic—neatly, but not too neatly—and handed these to Mr. Smythe.

"And one other thing to mull over for three to six months," he finished. "You recall the Orange County scandals. If we make a mistake, then you've accepted poor advice, but your advisory costs are minimized, and because we are independent there is no risk of a morality acceleration that could lead to scandal. In other words, no shit, no fan. If things go wrong, you still keep your job."

It was cramped in Smythe's office, because of the space taken up by an extra-large box of T-shirts next to where Jeff was sitting. Just the same, he felt marginalized after Jimmie took charge, and tried to alter his disposition through small talk. "Are these your kid's Little League team's T-shirts?"

Upon closer inspection, though, there was no wedding ring on his finger, and printed on the shirts was a compromising photo and matching quote of a presidential candidate. "On second thought, I have a friend in D.C. I'd like to hook you up with." How embarrassing.

I jumped in with quickly-summoned clichés. "Jimmy, I'm only the brains behind the operation here, but I have to say you're really thinking outside the box!"

"That's where I'm one step ahead of you," he beamed. "As far as I'm concerned, there is no box."

Mr. Smythe nodded expressionless throughout. We bid our *adioses* and departed his office politely but formally.

As we left, we noticed a group of four identikit bluesuits in the waiting room, seemingly standing in pecking order. Though I obviously had a burning comment, I thought better of it and held it 'til we were in the elevator. My peeve? These folks carry business cards promising 'professional advisor,' but given the level of industry automation, call-center beanies could perform many of the highly-paid jobs.

"It's good you kept your mouth shut before," Jeff warned. "They have to be the competition. They had 'the look.'" He then imitated perfectly their facial expressions. Imagine if the four advisors-in-waiting were picturing how Rodin would sculpt them sitting in the waiting room, and each was mimicking this appearance. How else do I describe *the look*?

Then I let fly toward Jimmy. "Why'd you let him off the hook? You had extra business cards from everyone in Fredovnic. Why did you scribble down his number in pig Latin?"

"Easy," he countered. "I thought if we hard sold in the first meeting, he'd be turned off. We forego the opportunity of a contract at the first crack, but I didn't think we had a quick-sale opening anyway. Some three to four months from now, after he's been fleeced by A.N. Other Investment Bank and belly-ached to Fredovnic, which is a lay-up trade for us, there's a long-term ticket waiting to be written. And by writing out Fredovnic's details by hand, it appeared spontaneous, even though I scripted the sequence."

I nodded, sensing a strategy that was well played. "Hi, ho!" I sighed. "You *could* sell Haagen-Dazs to the Danes."

Brilliant Colors

It was 3:45 PM that I snuck out of the office and walked into Reeves and Taylor Music, the converted shack tucked behind Bagels on the Square and Granite City Cleaners, on Second Avenue. Many times I've been convinced the owners should change their business status to museum, or charge a cover at the door. With a browse at your leisure policy, it seems to attract dozens of aficionados with no intention of making a purchase. Headphones for shoppers to listen to samples, and at some stations dual headphones so that friends can enjoy the same rarity concurrently. My eyes scanned the aisles with enthusiasm and I made eye contact with one of the owners. He looked back with an expression that acknowledged my appreciation of his efforts.

Big Sid joined me about five minutes later, grinning and carrying a pair of sports bottles. He spiraled one toward me and I caught it with an outstretched hand. I took a slug of my rye & ginger, nodded approval and grinned as well. Big Sid cradled his tequila sunrise.

After the secret handshake, Sid grabbed a few records and walked over to his usual station. A few minutes later, his head could be seen bopping to the beat. Sid is genuine, and always armed with a tonic of pop wisdom, even if he can't shake his fascination with doo-wop. In his side pocket was a paperback copy of *The Dharma Bums*. At the least, he is true to form.

I found the Experimental aisle and greedily eyed a vinyl original of "Little Sparrow," an unusual combination of late-60s psychedelics, symphonies and neon. My thumbs fumbled for a moment as I struggled to work the turntable. I closed my eyes and listened.

The combination spurred me to find the nearest female and hold her hand. Instead, my mind wandered to Patty, the girl whose smile could melt me a thousand times over. In my mind, I knocked on the door of her apartment and seconds later, she opened it. My arrival was not anticipated, but she opened the door excitedly regardless. I was carrying a bottle of champagne, a box of chocolates and a bunch of flowers. No, I was carrying two headphones and we listened to "Little Sparrow" together, harmoniously. The song ended and I opened my eyes. She was gone.

Big Sid was still digging, but he'd thankfully discarded the doo-wop and was now listening to bop. I found a couple swing records, and listened for a few spirited minutes, until the clarinets began to remind me of work.

At 4:30 PM, I handed my sports bottle back to Sid. He grinned and reminded me, "Sin's a good man's brother...if you catch my drift."

I caught his drift, but didn't think he knew the subtlety of the expression. Still, we weren't here for a behavioral debate. "Watcha find?" I asked.

He displayed two albums of the soul-before-it-was-called-that era, and raised his eyebrows. "How about you?" he asked.

"No, not today," I admitted. "But I can't remember the last time I've been able to relax for this long."

The Conference Call

Previous attempts to establish an independent political party that could seriously contend in national elections were based around the neo-populism and financial resources of a single individual, rather than the ideas, spirit and organization of a unified group. These prior attempts fizzled when the enamel fell off the single individual.

Our effort, the Movement, would succeed if we were able to design policies which would benefit a significant majority of the general public; we would fail if we were unable to assure this same group that we were acting in its interests. It would be an uphill struggle to convince the potential electorate that leaders of a political party were not "in it for themselves," even though transparently we weren't. And to succeed, we needed a focused core membership. Clear waters would make for fine sailing; likewise, keels take unkindly to bumps in the road.

Tony, founder and leader of the Movement, invited me to join after a dialogue he hosted at his think tank. The meeting was early Tuesday morning after a long weekend. We were the first to arrive in the building, which implied the heating had not yet been turned on. My first comment was, "let this be the first time I pray that a meeting be full of hot air!" Tony forced a slight smile, but did not otherwise hold the wisecrack against me. But I digress.

I later observed that the country had functioned best with a center-left Executive, center-right Congress, and moderate, open-minded Supreme Court. But what was the probability, I asked, that such an alignment would occur naturally, and what are the chances that the current power structure would tolerate such a favorable configuration for long? I then proceeded to describe an optimal ideological orientation for various arrays of agencies and bureaucracies at federal and regional levels.

After a short ponder, he responded, "I know of only a handful of people fascinated by this cogent yet undemonstrative field of analysis, but so many millions rely on and care about the outcome. Therefore, it's up to us to realign the constellation."

He then said, "We have an inherent advantage, which is that we know how to target what will be the next sought-after demographic: The

Zwieback and Sangria crowd of empty nesters and young grandparents."
I didn't know whether to knit my eyebrows, sneer or smile, but
acknowledged that he could be right.

Before enlisting, I was curious to know about the funding of the
Movement, which he assured me was limited, but diverse and sufficient.
Separately, I needed comfort that the organization was not merely an
inconspicuous front for another special interest. I took on faith the
sincerity of his body language and eye contact. It would not start the
relationship on the finest of first steps, after all, if I demanded a copy of
the Certificate of Incorporation.

Six of us were waiting on the phone line, from six different locations.
As co-head of strategy, it was my responsibility to generate ideas,
formulate policies, consider direction for the Technocrats who were the
public face of the Movement, and critique policies of the main parties. I
didn't have responsibilities for marketing or p.r.—someone else could take
my words or ideas and make them eloquent—or organization, although
occasionally I was involved in interviewing for new senior appointments.
I often wondered whether my dedication to this job, and the requirement
to constantly critique the work and habits of others, meant that I came
across as negative or closed-minded to the rest of the real world. However
undesirable this impression, I concluded that subordination to the needs
of the Movement was overriding and consideration of the perceptions of
others could wait.

The conference call was still about five minutes from starting, and
I was dwelling on the program "Fahrenheit 409" that I heard on the car
radio that morning. Well, I don't mind right-wing talk radio as much
as the left-wing variety, because while they both outdo their stereotype,
the right-wingers more frequently rely on common sense and emphasize
items of broader relevance, and less frequently come across as angered
unfocused energy. The goal of left-wing radio seems to be "taking back
power" and running the country the way the left ran it in the late '70s.
I don't know if they understand that we can't go back to tax and spend,
tax and spend, tax and spend, forever and without end, amen. However,
I wouldn't be waiting for this conference call to begin if I had a lot of
common ground with either party. There's more to serving our country
than drinking three lattes, or three Coors, and prancing in front of a
mirror, or puffing out your chest.

But I could not have anticipated the vitriol that had streamed from right-wing radio a short while earlier. Anomalously, the caller was talking about foreign policy, but not about the "usual suspects," so to speak, and was daring to deviate from the middle of the bell curve. He steered clear of claims we had already heard thousands of times before. Thank goodness for small favors.

I knew enough about Central American politics, but not so much about fashionable British popular music. Did 1980s English sophisticates really find fashion in advocating the political views of the Clash, some of whose lyrics loosely endorsed the Sandinistas, the regime that cratered Nicaragua into the second-poorest economy in the Western Hemisphere? Was it genuinely trendy to believe this band was as influential to the 1990s social revolution, and as helpful, as Poland's Solidarity?

Is it possible there was an abnormal but true U.N. accommodation of the Khmer Rouge, a strange but true understanding between then-Mayor Blacques Jacques Chirac and the Ayatollah Khomeini? Would Iran be a democratic, egalitarian and prosperous state, and the rest of the Middle East that much more stable, if not for Carter's misguided defense of the Shah at his tail end, and his take-it-personally conduct during the embassy hostage crisis? These claims seemed too fantastic to be true, too conspiratorial, yet I was not well-enough schooled in political history to judge the circumstantial assertions.

When I was convinced the right-wingers could not become any more confrontational, "Fahrenheit 409" host Cob Deuver summed up his show with a sermon about the 'new liberal talk-snuff offerings' and raised the question of whether these 'excitable Liberals' had ever promoted a productive idea, or whether Liberalism was mainly about projecting an image of squeaky clean and ten minutes after they were done foaming, there was a stubborn film that needed to be wiped clean with painstaking and repeated effort. They want to regain power so they can invoice the *foie gras* and the limousines back to the taxpayer. He closed the hour by concluding that the only solution to America's ailments was to seal the nation's borders and enact legislation making English the official language.

I had been tempted to lean right, but then I shook myself and recalled that both sides could play this game all day long—indeed, it is one of their focal games. This is not what *we* were about. We couldn't get sucked into it and I couldn't get sucked into it. Right-wing talk radio was compelling in a way, and provocative perhaps, but shock and awful definitely.

Then the conference call began, with Tony performing the kickoff.

"We have two items on the agenda today. First, we plan to hire a Communications Director over the next weeks. I've narrowed the list to three, and I'd like everyone to spend 60, 90 minutes with each at an early convenience. These are the criteria that I zeroed in on when I assembled the list: breadth of vision and style, self-motivation, ability to narrowcast, and discretion—until we publicly launch the Movement. I don't think that when you do speak you'll need to worry about whether or not to reveal parts of our strategy, as long as you use *your* discretion.

"At the same time, the interview process is not a one-way street; we need to impress the merit of joining forces with us, the criticality of remembering that each of us has an important but narrow role to play, and the possibility that he will have to lead a discreet life until the launch. Still, we need to retain the respect of the two we do not choose. We can't count on future loyalty, because we can't offer by hint the keys to the executive washroom one day, and admit the plumbing is broken and would they mind sharing the piss-pot with the enlisted men the next. With that in mind, each has the skills to do the job; the answer will come down to which can perform most effectively with the rest of the team as currently exists. I've emailed all the contact details. Please report back to me as and when. Make that when.

"The second topic is a little more sensitive, a little more awkward." He paused for a breath. "We need to do something about Hardin Cramer. He needs to be replaced as Figurehead, quickly, and we need to hope… need to hope he finds a TV weatherman job outside a top 20 media market. Those of you who want to focus on the past, recriminate, fine, but get this over quickly, because I will not let our project be derailed by an unwise, reversible hiring decision.

"We need to find someone else who knows how to use the energy of a crowd to his, ahem, to our benefit. Problem is, Hardin can work a crowd, but oh how a crowd can work him, too.

"Finding an appropriate replacement could take time, but there's no hurry; the Communications Director takes precedence. However, it is necessary to disassociate ourselves from Cramer gently and quickly. This will be difficult because of the promises he perceives to have received. If we don't do this right, there's no question in my mind that he will make the kind of bombastic noise we can do without. With that, the floor is open to suggestions."

This was serious. The Movement was imperiled and faced appropriation. Hardin Cramer was not the Big Garut most of us thought he was. Not the charismatic Figurehead we had in mind to attract attention to the Movement, allowing our policies and their implementation to then take over, but an undiluted megalomaniac. This was an unambiguous illustration of the negative happenstance of populist charisma, which would nullify the efforts of all unless he was dislodged swiftly.

Jerry decided to speak. "Listen. I've been out of the loop for a while. On what basis do we believe Hardin is not fit for the role as Figurehead?"

Tony was quick to reply. "With his actions, I feel he demonstrates a belief that he is larger than the Movement, will feel empowered to make policy decisions without consulting the appropriate functional areas of responsibility, and won't back off when I tell him to. But let this not be my decision. Does anyone disagree?"

Silence.

Tony once said about a high-profile politician from another party: "If I see him on *Meet the Press* or boasting that he's identified a solution to clean the campaign finance system, I'm gonna puke. If I see both, I'm gonna dry heave."

The silence continued for half a minute. "If we don't do this soon," Tony continued, a little fretfully, "we're playing for pride." Though his comments were amusing, no one dared laugh. Still, knowing his lateral thought patterns, I felt I could communicate his intentions.

I decided to open the blinds. "So what do you think, Tony? Is he worse than your friendly neighborhood Militant Submissive Communist?"

"Who's that?" Mark asked through a serious snicker. I sensed relief in his voice. Though I took an instant dislike to Hardin—at least this did me the small favor of saving time—Mark had worked with him.

Tony was pressed for time, and aggravated, but he was willing to expound on one of his many well-formulated theories for the other participants. I assumed political media manipulation was a 20th century phenomenon until Tony informed me that this was invented in

Peloponnesus in the fourth century B.C. I responded to this tidbit by exclaiming, "The Peloponnesians have a lot to answer for!"

Tony's political philosophy was guided by the writings of Friedrich Hayek, the early 20th century economist whose Nobel Prize was awarded for his understanding of organizational behavior and resource allocation. To the man on the street, though, he could be described as the founder of applied modern economics. Hayek was a pioneer on the impact of industrialization on everyday lives. Tony, like Hayek, had excellent mind-eye coordination when it came to common sense. His skill in interpreting the past was unsurpassed, as was his ability to read five or ten years into the future, though sometimes he wasn't the best judge of first impressions.

With a prophetic glint in his eye that only a seasoned shell game dealer could match, Tony revealed that centralized planning was discredited less than fifteen years ago, yet because of the transition costs, selected groups ignorantly want to bring it back. He then epitomized the militant submissive communist as "a member of the new far left who avidly supports the concept of centralized socialism, fully understanding the economic stagnation and social repression this produces, even though he is aware that he stands no chance of walking in the corridors of power should centralized socialism return. He will extract pleasure in being repressed. He sincerely hopes and believes he will trigger a starter's pistol on an upcoming tragic race to the bottom."

Cob Deuver was now on my mind, and I proceeded as if interrupted. "Hardin's worse than a limousine liberal. He's a fire-inhaling opportunist. I never liked him from the start."

So did Tony. "In more generous terms, the MSC prefers a society of equality, even with low living standards. He abhors the concept of inequality, even if this is consistent with the elimination of poverty."

"Why don't you take over as Figurehead, Tony?" Mark debated.

"It doesn't appeal," he admitted. "I don't want both roles and I don't think I'm capable of fulfilling the new role adequately. In any case, were it to come to that, it could be considered in due course. A first priority is to address the politics of Hardin."

"It's agreed we're in danger, but how are we gonna get him?" Mark exposited aloud.

"How?" another voice joined. "I see three choices. We can wait until he falls under his own weight; we can find a smoking gun; or we can play dirty."

"The bigger they are, the harder they fall," Armin joked. "Hardin has made himself unpopular in the past few weeks, Jerry's conscientious objection apart."

The sound of Jerry placing his glasses on his desk was audible through the loudspeakers. He couldn't see and speak at the same time, bless him. Meanwhile, though, he didn't like the idea of appearing the softie, so he consequently horselaughed: "The problem is, Hardin thinks he's a sexual intellectual, when in reality he's a FUCKING idiot!" ·

Raucous laughter of approval followed, causing Tony to stifle a hoot and audibly clear his throat. The phone line then went as quiet as Centre Court.

"I've seen every episode of the Sopranos. Let's find his weak spot," Armin signaled. "Mike could find a way to achieve our objective," he predicted.

A dull silence ensued.

"Mike's dead," Tony announced.

"Jesus, no..." Armin blurted, and then his voice trailed off.

I broke the silence by insisting, "I'm finding the gun."

"The other two tactics could be more effective...," one listener started.

"And quicker," another finished.

"I'm finding the gun," I redoubled.

"Okay, I'll give you three weeks," Tony agreed, after contemplation. "To be honest, I don't genuinely think there is an alternative, and I don't know how I'd promulgate an alternative without damaging our reputation over the longer run. I hope it's not a busy time for you at the office. Let me know if you need additional resources."

Tony created this monster, but I didn't mind fixing it. I could be vicious and ruthless—when necessary—and because of my image as polite and bookish, I could often get away with certain actions without suspicion or attribution. Moreover, though it would satisfy me immensely to be responsible for Hardin's tipping over, I felt no need for public acclamation. Thus, I was a wise selection as hatchet man.

What if the opposition dug deep on me, I wondered suddenly, and panicked. What would they find? I exhaled, and relaxed. I'm not running for anything, I reminded myself.

Jimmy Takes a Call

Jeff and I were chatting aimlessly in front of the coffee machine when Jimmy strode over excitedly.

"Boys, it looks like we owe Fredovnic a large one the next time we're in the Midwest!"

"Why?" Jeff joked, "Did he give you an inside edge at the track?"

"No. Remember when I bluffed Ruritania? It turns out he and Fredovnic are chums and frequently share notes as it is. Ruritania checked us out almost immediately. Fredovnic told him not to bother with the other clowns, as one set of clowns would do. Just kidding. He agreed each advisor could do the job, but we would be no less effective, and would definitely be cheaper and, more importantly, easier to deal with. He trusts us to give a simple answer to a simple question...for example."

So much for being concerned about the 'the look.'

"Such a deal. Why didn't Smythe say they're on each other's speed dials?" Jeff asked.

"He wanted to see whether we really had the contract with Fredovnic," Jimmy replied, "or bluffed with information from the city's website."

"That's nothing," I proclaimed. "I once secured a job as a corporate advisor after looking up names of 'likely' companies to apply to in the Yellow Pages."

"You're joking!" Jeff expressed in disbelief. "Did they ask how you became aware of the firm?"

"Yeah, I said it was in a directory with listings of every top-tier company...hey, I was telling the truth!" I maintained. "It was a strange company. There were two *pro bono* directors and another who paid for the shelf space..."

"Another time!" Jimmy interrupted. "We were talking about Ruritania!" He wasn't using his inside voice, but we guessed this was because he feared Jeff and I had many more lame jokes in reserve, rather than because he was genuinely angry.

"Oh, yeah," Jeff said apologetically. "This is the coffeemaker we were hearsaying in front of, not the water cooler," which meant a lack of undivided attention was out the question. "What's the bottom line? That he was bluffing you too?"

"Well, yes," he indicated, with bashful pride. "That and I already signed and faxed back the contract. We gotta return there next month to collect data for his upcoming fiscal year's financing preview."

Yet I looked apprehensive, and it showed. "Don't look so excited," Jimmy said, with attempted sarcasm. "I said we won the *deal*!"

I had to think of a bluff of my own. I paused. Well, I always have a lame joke *and* a bluff in reserve. "I didn't want to mention this before," I admitted, "but I didn't think our chances were so strong after...you see, I once had a running argument, for about nine months, with someone who works down the corridor from Smythe. I saw his name plate on an office door when we were there for the presentation. I thought our proposal was going to turn out a lost cause."

Yet Jimmy had a visage of relaxation on his face. "One of the first rules of business," he explained, "is never assume that people in the same company talk to each other."

"I'll remember that. My last negative question, then, is: if we foul up one of them, will we sacrifice both contracts? Did that come out right?"

He thought about this for a few seconds. "No, it didn't, but if either project is unsuccessful, then we just have to find a way for all to save face...and we still get *paid*!"

"So," Jeff asked me, "what *were* you planning to do this weekend?"

"Ah," I stumbled. "I had tickets for Bob Sherman's irreverent new exposé about Wall Street."

"Bob Sherman," he hmmed, "isn't he...?"

"Yeah, *Musical Chairs*, that Bob Sherman. Some critics depict him as the master of the absurd, but I like his talent for the tragicomedy. I suppose I'll give the tickets to my sister."

Jimmy's bluff was unnecessary in the end, as Ruritania knew of us all along and simply wanted to ensure we had sufficient poise not to jab it during the pitch, or be distracted by his picture window view of the mountains. Moreover, this was bread-and-butter, and there was little chance we'd sully the opportunity. The worst-case scenario was that Smythe suspected we sold below cost to "buy the business," to list him as a bow string for our modest but growing track record. That was Jimmy's biggest worry. Mine was that there were only going to be 24 hours per day over the next month, and that included the six I'd budgeted for sleeping.

The Interview

"It's like this. The major parties are proficient at: raising money, spending it, making commercials, going on the attack, creating 'messages' and sound bites. This is running a campaign, how they compete against the rival and the *modus operandi* of congress, but it's not an efficient way to run the country. The first thing we'll do is neutralize the lobbyists. There are capable academics and bureaucrats to advise and write legislation without resorting to intermediaries who introduce hurdles, raise costs and prevent businesses from generating competitive advantage through innovation and elbow grease.

"It is imperative that we reshape the tax system, especially the corporate tax system, to upgrade equity and efficiency. Corporate tax rates have been brought to too low a level, and personal income payers suffer too great a burden. We will streamline the system and emphasize user fees, so that the incidence of a tax falls on those who use and can afford a public service. Furthermore, we will eliminate subsidies to non-viable companies. If I give you, a corporation, a subsidy, then you give me, the taxpayer, a stake in that corporation if you fail to repay the subsidy. This is our money, after all." I consciously borrowed that phrase from Jimmy.

"We recognize, though, that corporate taxes have to be relatively low, stable and predictable, because companies with healthy after-tax incomes are healthy job creators. Reflecting the empire-building tendencies in today's modern corporation, there might even be a tendency to over-hire when profitability rises. We should therefore exploit corporate psychology, to the extent possible, to maximize employment creation.

"Now, we've got how many tax lawyers and accountants prowling the land for a quick and easy buck? Rhetorical question. If they provide a real service, good for them. However, if their aim is to split the difference between the letter and spirit of the law, disdainfully believing there is neither the will nor the administrative capacity to challenge them, or where corporations are sneaky enough to hire ex-IRS senior employees as 'I scratch your back' insurance, we will set examples. Transportation subsidies must be overhauled, but not even I understand them yet.

"By the way, this is not the voice of an *angry* strategist for the opposition, but rather a *focused* strategist for the opposition. My motto is 'positive focused energy.'" We both chuckled lightly.

"The political parties in our midst are consumed with 1) getting reelected, and 2) placating their interest groups. The necessary-evil part of organizing a bureaucracy is to them an end in itself, rather than a means to an end. We need to raise the efficiency of government and shrink the cost of running it. Studies have shown that for every 1% reduction in *ordinary* government spending, a 1.3% increase in capital investment ensues. Yes, that's right. If we rationalize public spending, the economy gets 30% for free! And it's not difficult; it's not *card counting*. Now, imagine if government gets swift and finds a way to cut *wasteful* spending.

"We don't want to eliminate all the pork-barrel spending, because who is to say we shouldn't allocate untied funds to congressmen to spend wholly in their districts, at their discretion? Who is to say this is unfair, unnecessary or undesirable? However, I say let's do this, but let's do it transparently, without the pretending. By opening the process, though, the non-recipients of the largesse will become aware of whom they crassly subsidize and hopefully the outrage will, let's say, streamline the practice."

This was supposed to be an interview, but as it was clear that I loved my secondary job—and he was intrigued by the Movement and my transparency—he was content to let me continue. However, it was time for a break, and thus we agreed to resume the discussion over lunch. I was momentarily blown back by one of his requests, but calmed down when I remembered this was a man with young children. Such a pleasant and capable publicist, I concluded over the ensuing half-hour, but would our demands for devotion and discretion prove a double-edged long straw? What well-grounded family man would reject a safe haven of eight-hour workdays and ten-hour nights of baby talk, first steps, and dropped bottles for the manic self-confinement which was the Movement?

A few slabs of olive bread later though, my blood sugar was above normal and I was anxious to continue with my policy foundation.

"This sounds great, doesn't it, but how can we make inroads? No other legislative system embeds such incumbency. This contradicts the desires of the population. Our basic theory is that people want to vote, but also want self-respect at the ballot box. Consider that only about half the eligible population votes. In one recent national election, more than 50% did stay home. The two main parties split the rest, after corralling many reluctant voters. This gives us close to 60% to work with. A few sparks will provide the momentum we need. The Great Disregarded will wonder why we waited so long.

"Ours is an untested party, so we know not to overstate the size of the pie. Our base case scenario gives us 23% within six years, though we'd settle for 15%, certainly enough to tilt the balance of power. Without proportional representation, we'd be less visible in Congress, but there is no question we'd have a mandate to steer change. The risk to our long-term survival is that the duopolists adopt—adapt, steal, whatever—our centrist, waste-averse policies, which we doubt because of their tendency to mean-revert toward the special interest. That would be a blessing: if the major parties acted with the public's interest in mind, there would be no need for us in the first place.

"Virtually every policy is on a pendulum, but the major parties attempt to shift it to where along the axis they would prefer, rather than where the public interest dictates and requires. Still, we recognize that the private sector is generally more efficient at providing goods and services, and can resolve most of its problems, so we try to avoid forcing a solution. For the most part, the country benefits when the morass that is our political system drives talented people away from public service; their skills can be more effectively deployed in the private sector. But politics has become too important to be left to the politicians."

I called for another break. My mind was drifting and I realized the previous several minutes would have been more effective if pre-worded. That, and I was daydreaming. I recalled the Washington Muni Finance conference and the DNC pep rally. The eager twenty-somethings seemed a different world away. Why did I find it so much easier to live lighter in my real job, and why did I treat a hobby as do or die? Nonetheless, I recovered from break point down by signalling the intermission via pretend baby talk and patching him on the shoulder. I hadn't yet explained my view of his role, and with this homily in mind I spiked his cappuccino with an extra shot before we began the closing stretch, hoping he was a coffee achiever.

"A division leader must be immersed in a policy topic distinct from his forte, because of the tendency for single-issue specialists to lose perspective, and to think that if you know one issue thoroughly, you know everything. In our view, diversity is the spice of effective government. Finally, we have—don't laugh—a professor of unintended consequences. This, as it turns out, is one of our more important roles. We don't recommend a particular policy if the positive repercussions are outweighed by negative consequences elsewhere, just the same if a proposal does not pass the 'so what' test.

"We won't rely on expensive TV attack commercials, and so we won't need huge money or a gigantic staff. The Movement was designed to thrive with a streamlined infrastructure, and vice versa. Moreover, we will not respond to attack ads. If such tactics backfire, then so be it. Admittedly, inexperience is our electoral vulnerability. Not that we won't have the skills to legislate; rather, that our Candidates are untested. We need Candidates who will represent our—in other words, the electorate's—interests, rather than their own, but power corrupts and blah, blah, blah. Well, we've conducted voter surveys and know already which will be our key battlegrounds, but I've already gored you with too much minutiae.

"And since this is an interview, what in my view are we looking for in a communications director?

"We have about 12 key policy areas—don't quote me on the exact number—including domestic and international economics, Social Security, regulatory policy, the military, health, education, energy, Social Security, etcetera. We need to produce a chapter for each, including a one-paragraph summary, an outline, and a detailed strategy. The job of the communications director is to coordinate these chapters, ensure they are consistent, and disseminate the relevant components to constituents, the media, and so on, when appropriate, and to organize briefing sessions for the division chief with the media, public policy research groups, etcetera. If the division chief is not capable of immediately describing his endeavors in ordinary language, it would be your job to translate for the layman. Clearly, we have to be able to explain our positions extremely well. We've set a lot of bars quite high.

"We're content to provide the level of detail an outsider requests, but we won't prioritize less-meaningful sound bites over detailed analysis. We have no control freaks, but, for example, anyone who uses disturbing platitudes such as 'we will work hard to improve relations with the international community' will be in big trouble. 'Mass appeal, not crass appeal.' That one I like, though.

"There's scope to work closely with the technical support staff. This aspect of the job is part internal, part external. How do we inform Tony what the data are saying and how do we explain the raw data to the outside world? But much of this is still to be fleshed out. As I mentioned, we have statisticians very capable of interpreting data and interacting with the internet gurus. Information wants to be opaque.

"We'll take on a few more webmasters, linear programmers and the like. We keep them locked in a room next door to the other overly-committed faithful we call the Museum of Purists."

He laughed and I responded. "The question I know you're dying to ask: there is no Museum of the Seen to be Seen Doing. They thankfully work for the other sides. It seems to work better for everyone that way.

"So, how does this sound?"

On the way out, he grinned and man-hugged me. I grinned too, because the three of us successfully accomplished this interview, Tony included, in spirit and intent. I gratefully reciprocated his well-meant gesture, though I'm not a man-hugger by nature.

The International Business Trip, or, Leave Your Delusional Left-Wing Anger with the Coat-Check Girl

There was a pile of records and tapes strewn loosely around my living room floor, waiting for a compilation CD to be burned. Included were several out-of-print recordings lent by Big Sid, my hidden gem collaborator, and on top of the pile was *The Hits of the Bronzeadatura Improv Club*, the outmost-of-print of all.

Our increasingly frequent business travel would be more tolerable, I reasoned, with musical montages to our muni finance strategy roadtrips: "pairing music," as an ironic friend of mine calls it. Radio stations have evolved and there is now a channel for every taste, but "no commercial interruptions indeed" is still wishing upon a star, and thus my volunteering to burn ones for the road.

Prematurely, therefore, the phone call directive to attend a conference in London occurred with logical sequences in my head; records, tapes and CDs on the floor; and the CD writer empty. The conference churned out a professional waste of time, because British cities and counties are not permitted to raise money on their own behalf—anymore. A couple of the wealthier local councils undertook financial engineering in 1987 and took a bath when markets moved against them, but found a judge to issue an Indonesia-style ruling that they entered into these contracts without proper legal authority. The investment banks and merchant bankers—who ostensibly lived in these well-heeled neighborhoods—ended up soaked with the losses instead.

Shortly thereafter, the councils' borrowing wings were clipped. They could still spend money the central government apportioned them out of general tax revenues any way they saw fit—and why fix the schools when you can hire a dozen political-correctness police and build potholes that would make Canal Street in Manhattan green with envy? But they could not issue bonds, and so there were no British local authorities for us to advise. There was a burgeoning market on the Continent, but we'd have to learn the financial culture of the country first and employ more bilingual staff, and that business plan evolution was at least two years away. Don't walk before you can swim.

Nonetheless, there were opportunities to conduct research for my second job. This was a particularly sensitive period in the United Kingdom, especially for visiting Americans. I'd read in the internationally-oriented press that anti-American sentiment was rampant throughout Western Europe, but I didn't hear an ungracious word from any of the non-British conference delegates. I could agree or disagree with an opinion without being forced to like or dislike the person on the basis of that opinion. They were unapologetic when they felt strongly about an issue, but they raised their concerns with civility and without feeling the need to threaten. Perhaps they were the rules that proved the exception, but on the whole, the truism about widespread unpopularity and distrust of Americans by Western Europeans appeared to be a myth. Distressingly, few foreign media persons have been brave or diligent enough to uncover it.

Bizarrely enough, the French were the friendliest and the English the most stubborn. Presumably it was the conference location, but when townies in areas adjacent to the arena heard my accent, it proved *carte blanche* to lay into me. Narrow minded, not interested in facts, "neo-coms," I thought to myself. These were the real militant-submissive communists. Our American left-wingers couldn't hold a candle to these Stalinist masochists.

The English and their villages are of good repute in the U.S., and many Americans have relatives "across the pond" who are spoken of with admiration: Britpop movies and music solidified the conventional reputation. The only warning I received was about English-passport-holding "Eurotrash." Thus, being new to the country, one particular dialogue was loudly against the grain and un-anticipatable. I should have known by the "Bliar Out of Chechenya" and "SABE" (Students Against Bloody Everything) T-shirts that you couldn't win an argument with these hobgoblins: a logical and rational conversation cannot be pursued with someone whose idea of a rebuttal is to revert to Little-Red-Book-isms.

"What's on your mind?" I asked congenially.

"The 'war,'" he replied angrily, as if I'd been scoffing him.

"What war?" I asked, and pointed out with dismay the many civil wars and cross-border conflicts currently ongoing, some of which were proving particularly brutal and intractable.

Then he "reminded" me that *his* was the only real war, as if those I mentioned had been filmed in Arizona, next door to the since-abandoned lunar landing soundstage. It seemed that also, according to his knowledge set, press reports of slaughter in the conflict countries I described were figments of a right-wing director's imagination, at the behest of a crooked media, which have been scripted but not yet filmed.

He knew the truth and derivation of these conflicts at least as well as me, I was convinced. He wouldn't be volunteering his opinions self-confidently to a random public audience if he didn't. I was further convinced his one-sidedness was designed to limit debate. His was a battle of ideas, and if alternative opinions were not aired, he couldn't lose the vote, in his view. I was willing to have a candid discussion about ideological and religious tolerance, history book rewriting and the ability of closed societies to cope with democracy for the first time. If I can learn something from a stubborn character with a narrow point of view, mutual aversion can take a back seat and the Movement can thank me later. My naivety and his ignorance sunk in only gradually.

Much of the new protest community has nostalgia for the slogans that survived the Vietnam War era and believes present circumstances are comparable, but the protesters will only substantiate the words on their placards if they reveal an ability to think as loudly as they shout. It's easier to say "Stop the War" than to understand what unfair merchandise trade regimes and economic moral hazard are, or concede that developing countries are shooting themselves in the foot with their own unenlightened economic policies.

The world is worse than ever, the Angry's for the Sake of Being Angry (ASBAs) say, yet China and Vietnam have seen the light and dropped low standards of living as a policy goal, South Africa is democratic, and less than 20% of the Latin population lives under truly hopeless, corrupt or dictatorial regimes. Until 15 years ago, the percentage was close to 100%. Russians, despite their hindrances, can travel and surf the Internet at will.

But this is not enough for the ASBAs, who have no capacity for understanding how debilitating for society conscription was, and remains where it still exists. Banishing the draft in the U.S. was a major accomplishment, lest we forget it once existed.

"It is necessary to fight inequality and injustice for their own sake," I explained unemotionally, "and because they are responsible for producing many, varied forms of domestic violence. However, there is no strong link between inequality and cross-border violence. Mostly the origin is clear cut; for instance, land grabs, ethnic clashes, or unwillingness to coexist peacefully with dissimilar neighbors. Hence, when you assert an untenable emotional link, you willfully create new misunderstandings and allocate blame ineptly."

It was a hopeless attempt to educate the ASBA about the real conflicts in Europe, Africa and the Middle East, where thousands were dying each month thanks to cynical actions by governments and their militias, and deliberate self-congratulatory inaction amid unanimous expressions of shock/horror by the United Nations.

"These are complicated issues," he blathered. "The genocidal government is doing its best...You're just prejudiced against the Arabs... It's not nearly as bad as you say...The West is exploiting the leaders by buying their oil at record prices...You're exaggerating the numbers...I change the subject," and so on. In the 21st century, you *can* fight City Hall, but you *can't* fight the new political correctness.

I discussed this altercation with a laid-back Dutch delegate who had spent several years in the Middle East. "What do you expect to happen in the land of the blind?" he asked rhetorically. In his view, though, worse than the ASBA are aid agency administrators working in developing countries who have "gone local." He spoke of one outwardly effervescent young woman, working overseas on extended contracts, who "became vile" when the subject turned to politics. It was natural for her to prescribe conservative Islamic law penalties on practitioners of political incorrectness. Those who repressed their population, while stealing economic opportunity from it, and those who militantly protested this behavior, were both preferable to the average American who supports his country's foreign policy.

I remained furious when I returned to the hotel—until half an hour later, when these dialogues helped me understand the wheat which was the opportunity that we in the Movement saw to extend the legacy of the Woodstock generation, and the chaff which was the distraction of the ASBAs. I needed to focus on the wheat and discard the chaff. Woodstock had made the world a better and fairer place. We consciously adopted the responsibility to take it to the next level. I virtually began to reach out, grab it and taste it.

My mind skipped to phone calls I hadn't returned. I wanted to tell Patty all of this; I wanted to tell her how close we were to tasting success. I forgot about work, work, work, and began to relive the strong hints she used to drop, how she would call to ask irrelevant questions, tell me how much she liked my handwriting. Very soon, I would be able to confide, both about the fount of my preoccupation all these months, and that I would soon have free time for her.

It had been a long day and my capacity for processing information rapidly diminished. It was time for distraction from these conflicting thoughts with a good night's sleep. Just as well, because a migraine was returning. As Big Sid once told me, everything radiates from the head, warmth up and out, personality down. I closed my eyes.

Shortly before awaking from a warm sweat in the middle of the night, I staggered through two delirious and one absurdist dream, which proceeded as follows:

In the first, I was sitting in a booth at a 24-hour coffee barn in California, with papers spread over the table, as I gathered evidence against Hardin. I pieced an ever-gathering array of evidence against him, until I finally put the puzzle together. Immediately, I called Mark, who in this dream was still working for Hardin. When he heard my explanation, he flung the cordless phone and raced into Hardin's office, jumping and skipping as if dancing on his grave.

Jump-cut to a nearby bar, where Hardin would often take employees for a dressing down, especially Mark. In this sequence, Mark and Hardin were sitting across each other at a table. Hardin excused himself to the men's room, and before he returned, Mark placed next to Hardin's drink a newspaper clipping of an axing of Hardin's counterpart at a rival firm for presumed incompetence, and mouthed the words, "Roll 'em." After Hardin sat down and saw the headline, Mark put his arm around his shoulder and hummed a recent popular song, "It Could Happen to You."

Jump-cut to the International Court of Justice in the Hague, where Tony Blair was being tried for assertions that certain countries were awash in weapons of mass destruction. His accuser was Charles Kennedy of the Liberal Democratic Party. If the court ruled against Mr. Blair, he would be forced to step aside, and Mr. Kennedy would accede into the vacated

Prime Minister's chair. Michael Howard, leader of the Tory Party *aka* the Loyal Opposition, was nowhere to be found.

The panel of judges asked the expert witnesses the findings of their detailed surveys: were any weapons of mass destruction uncovered?

"It was impossible to ascertain for sure," the leading forensic expert explained, "for it was difficult to excavate all possible sites, what with the obstructions caused by the mass graves—but, to the best of our knowledge, no, there were not."

This excited the leader of the Liberal Democrats, whose eyes became wickedly triumphant. "With all due respect, Mr. Blair," he beamed equally toward the defendant, the judges and the TV cameras, "you brought this country into war under the wrong pretences, and therefore you don't have a frog's chance in France of convincing the court that..."

And then, fortunately, I woke up, and stayed there motionless for the next four hours, until it was a reasonable hour to get out of bed.

Of the reasons I became involved with the Movement, I would often think sentimentally of friends growing up and recall their frustrations with the status quo. How the political fabric was sucking the public policy interest out of everyone, degenerating the national morale and sapping vital personal resources. The tune which then came into my head was a Motown instrumental, which became heartbreaking with the slightest change in inflection. They wanted someone to do something about it. I could! But if we didn't figure out how to jettison Hardin Cramer soon, he would bring the entire association down.

Thus, my feelings of being disconnected and disjointed, especially from 3,500 miles away. We had a project to start in California; there were friends whose aspirations about the future I promised to address; I had no champagne ideas about Cramer; and I was stuck over here with ASBAs who were pissing me off. Wake me up when *my* September ends, would someone?

I restlessly emailed colleagues in the Movement, but still Cramer was a puzzle whose pieces were in skew planes. I knew what a clumsy banker and business manager he had been, how he had shirked duties, micro-managed oppressively, flown first class unnecessarily, and time-managed haphazardly. However, these were not offenses we could merely remind him of and he would walk away. We couldn't say, "Sorry, you're not our man." He was stubborn and entrenched. His game was to ride on our tailwind and hope we had no trump card to pull, no smoking pistol to bluster.

It's no wonder that I was nervous, stressed and irritable, as I had six days to find the solution I fervently insisted I could deliver. I would not be home for two more days, and the day after that I would have to make tracks for California. Somehow I had to find time to prepare a PowerPoint presentation for the municipal bond department of Ruritania and color copies for everyone. It didn't seem like it was going to happen.

I'm Going to California, at Least That's What I'm Telling My Friends

Because I didn't finish the presentation on time, all the convenient flights had departed and I was forced to fly to an airport that was a four-hour's drive away.

While waiting to board, I called Mark in Chicago, my other initial ally in the Ditch Hardin Cramer faction. "How did we get into this mess?" I asked. We knew. Hardin had an ability to spout waffle and sound both profound and authoritative. Most people were taken in for long enough.

Allowing Hardin to become drafted as Figurehead was a mistake we let run out of control, one we could have vetoed if we'd moved quickly enough. Like many things, though, you often don't think of these things until it's too late. In an effort not to ruffle our otherwise perfect unity, we decided not to criticize Tony for nominating him. We agreed Hardin couldn't last through the launch process, and his selection would prove a harmless mistake at worst, and potentially a learning exercise at best. Moreover, we never guessed he'd be able to accumulate such leverage against the Movement.

I often thought of a conversation that Mark relayed about encounters he and other subordinates had with Hardin. After a particularly pointless dispute, Hardin would stop listening to facts and/or reason and shout, "Who the F are you?" Which, because of his size, would lead the victim to back away.

However, on one occasion Mark had had enough, and instead leaned in and screeched even more vocally, "No, who the F are you, halitosis breath!"

Despite the insult, Hardin flinched only for a moment. He then straightened and smiled, almost cruelly. He had a capacity to act as if he had the upper hand and was in control, under most circumstances, and this many observers misinterpreted as a symptom of strength.

We knew otherwise.

The irony, the severe irony, was that the launch plan for the Movement was well ahead of schedule. Developments could not have been proceeding more nicely. I had to find the smoking gun.

Brain waves in the air are different, more creative, than my brain waves on the ground. As I scanned the dark plains from 30,000 feet, my head was swimming with ideas of gleaming roads to the future. But all roads led to the spaghetti junction known as the resolution of the politics of Hardin Cramer and all road building would have to stop without this resolution. I had to find the smoking gun.

I arrived late at night in Salem, Oregon, picked up the rental car and headed south into Northern California. It was going to be a long ride, both time-wise and in consideration of all that was on my mind. I was futilely exhausted when I flicked on the radio and heard a commercial for daytime TV, in a rhyming tune:

Barney was a dinosaur,
His show was really boring,
Every time when people watch,
You can always see them snoring.

I wasn't hallucinating. It *was* a commercial, for a spoof comedy or a children's birthday party entertainer, but I didn't care to find out which. It was a sufficient hint to change the channel. The driving rain was sarcasm enough.

The radio heard my pleadings and played exactly the song I wanted to hear. Thank you, DJ.

I recalled my first trip to Northern California, some six years ago, and 45 minutes in the Panorama Bar of the Ruritania Marriott while I waited for my associates to run up their hotel room phone bills, freshen up, and slide into their casual duds. Though instead of cool brown ale and twilight game baseball, it was 45 minutes of wandering conversation with the Middle-Aged Daddy-O in a Cowboy Hat, with Aerolineas Goofy cartoons on the Galavision TV set in the background. "Buy the ticket, take the ride," he said, more than once. More than once.

This was Daddy-O heaven, the Panorama Bar, and whoever walked into his sphere of influence became a captive listener for at least 45, but it was also his Last Chance Saloon, his hell, because he can never leave. But if you look beyond the shoulder of the Daddy-O, you can picture through the window the early morning mowing and fresh dew, before the gardeners make way for the whistling chef to fire up his outdoor breakfast.

And if you look beyond the barbecue, you can with a little imagination visualize in the distance the crest of a great wave, upon which rose the ideals and expectations of a great many young people in decades past, before the waves broke, and rolled back.

Hi, ho. Has it really been six years?

One of these days, these projects would finish and I'd call the mental list of new and old friends to explain my invisibility and lack of communication. I was busy keeping my promise to the recipients of that unspoken pledge. How would Patty react to such a long delay in returning her calls? I had various reasons for wanting to speak with others, but with Patty I merely wished to share good news. That of the Movement was prospectively the best I could have. On how many occasions had she dropped hints of sincere interest and how consistently had I responded, sincerely, that I couldn't fit her into my schedule? Just the same, I dared not call if I had no news to report at all.

I looked at the three folders on the passenger seat, one the PowerPoint presentation for Ruritania, another the strategy documents for the next conference call of the Movement, and a third my unrelated and bland notes about Hardin. Floating by in a fourth, imaginary folder were images and voices of Patty. I pulsated affectionately and temporarily forgot about the rain and the folders.

However, they were stacked too high and couldn't be rebuffed. "This is what I am!" I reminded myself. "This is what I must do! I cannot be distracted now." I clearly could not picture myself dialing her number.

This diversion from heavy, albeit self-welcomed responsibilities, cleared my head and I was better able to concentrate on the immediate. And never underestimate the power of a song on the radio. It is amazing, perhaps even ironic, the damage that trivia can do. It is somewhat more impressive when trivia is important, but the trumpet call occurs when this trivia is useful to me.

Well, luckily I had a mind for trivia.

A pair of recollections intersected at that moment and I simultaneously recalled a sardonic comment that an old friend once made about Hardin and a photographic snapshot of his resume. Professor Shelton spoke sarcastically about Hardin because of his minimal effort in the professor's evening class at Golden State Community College. Hardin was desperately anxious to scare up an MBA, even if this was from a community college aimed at blue-collar overachievers, and even if he received a low passing grade. Shelton respected the greater part of the blue-collar student body, because MBA school was going to be a serious challenge for them, for reasons I'll defer until later. Hardin, though, attended this school only because he expected it would prove cheap and easy.

"No," I told myself triumphantly, "it doesn't say Golden State on his resume; it says UCal Berkeley."

I stopped the car at the next coffee shop along the highway and bought a drink to sip while considering this information. Yes, I'm positive about both these items. I'm distinctly positive about both. He won't be able to continue after we present the discrepancy to him. I removed my cell phone from an inside pocket and called Mark again, forgetting that it was two hours later there.

I'd woken him, so he didn't fully incorporate what I was announcing. Sleepy grogginess explained his seeming lack of attention, but what I had to share was too important.

"But everyone lies on his resume," he said in a daze. "Are you sure anyone is going to make a fuss?"

"It's not a white lie," I clarified. "There's a huge difference between Berkeley and Golden State. Besides, even if he had been honest, imagine anyone being taken seriously as a Player with a resume pinnacle such as that, especially with the pedigreed veneer he projects."

"It's over Hardin," my case closed, "go home." I was then overcome by a cloud nine grin. It was time to reopen the books on my own personal life.

Mark was convinced, but for him this could wait until the morning. "Good night then," I conveyed. "We can't press him to resign until we have the documentary evidence. I'll stay in California an extra day to call on the Golden State transcript department. I'm sure Professor Shelton will assist me." I wanted to organize a conference call with the other division chiefs immediately, but after speaking with Mark, agreed the good news could wait another day and a half.

Moreover, I needed to devote my attention to the next morning's meeting with Ruritania. If my colleagues and the finance director wondered why I arrived at these discussions in such a bright mood, despite my work overload and travel calamity, they might have deduced this was because I was excited to have an unanticipated new client with whom I could share my unique proprietary analytical methods. Although this was undeniably so, the main reason was, at that moment I realized for the first time that we were well on our way.

COLUMBUS DAY

"It's a small world, but it's not a hilarious world."
Bill Watterson

Before Sundown

It was a typical day in the life of Fran Obrien, fifteen months into a case that was approaching the make or break stage. He was standing on the roof of a Manhattan apartment building at dusk, admiring the colors as air particles mixed with reflections off the Hudson River. It was late winter, the kind of day in which the sky alone speaks that the new season is trying to break through.

The year was 1992, before cell phones, before the Internet, before hypertext, before Starbucks. When disco was still dead. In the land of the blind, ASCII text and Au Bon Pain were the one-eyed men. It was a time of great uncertainty, with renewed prosperity perpetually just around the bend, but it was also a great time to be a gourmet, because the previous autumn's harvest had been excellent.

Fran had spent an extended period traveling, and his mind was full of culinary ideas he was dying to replicate. There were items in his suitcase he had brought back expressly for experimenting in his kitchen. He infrequently went to the same country twice, the samples depleted quickly, and it was difficult to recreate the flavor with domestic substitutes. Oh, the trials of an amateur perfectionist.

Eat-to-live food in regular cities is tastier than so-called "innovative concoctions" in fashionable restaurants, Fran often reminded himself. *Haute cuisine*: do any everyday people really wear it? However, despite New York's reputation as a city in which you can source everything, Fran sensed a frustration that there were many ingredients he saw on his travels that were not available in Manhattan. Portuguese bacon. Peruvian roasting popcorn.

To occupy himself while traveling, Fran would play a game he called "A is for..." A is for Austria: one of his favorite humble Austrian foods was the autumn cranberry. Belgium: mountain ham. Canada: sharp Cheddar. Denmark: crispy fried onions. England: little gem lettuce. France: Normandy pears. And so on. In a second round, he would adorn his selection of the first round, and in a third, he would remind himself where he had tasted it or when he had prepared it at home.

The cooking wizardry took his mind off the tension of his cases, which were habitually intractable at the outset, thus allowing him to concentrate more fully when necessary. The converse was not true, though. There was never a bad time to think about a favorite dish or the possibility of a new one. His wife, Darby, approved of his hobby, and naturally her palate appreciated the results of his labors of love. The source of his great curiosity and imagination was mysterious, but he definitely inherited his culinary skill from his mother, who, ironically enough, preferred the classic Danube Basin dishes. And in contrast with his day job, cooking was definitely about the chase, not the capture.

New Street

He gazed to the west, toward the mighty Hudson, watched the sun reflect off the water and the aging, majestic skyscrapers and inhaled the cold, fresh air. "Amazing," he thought. "A view like this on all our doorsteps." Though he liked the way he must have appeared on the top of this building, pensive against a New York skyline, Fran accepted that it was time to descend and start work.

He opened the rooftop door deliberately and walked contemplatively down the seven flights of stairs. Seven is the maximum number of storeys that apartment buildings in the Village could hold without installing elevators at the time this structure was erected, and this trivia explains the height of many blocks in this section of the city.

Fran walked slowly southward until he reached the Wall Street district. It was only six, but the office towers were emptying rapidly. In this industry of early risers, many office workers kept seemingly blue-collar hours, departing shortly after the five o'clock bell to catch commuter trains to Jersey, the Island or Westchester. Soon, it would be only the investment banking departments and law firms where the oil still burned.

He walked past the Stock Exchange and turned right onto New Street, one of Southern Manhattan's narrowest and most obscure streets, but also one of the first he remembered from his teenage years. His parents would occasionally bring him, his brother and sister to this historic district to sightsee: the Stock Exchange, Federal Hall, and the Woolworth Building, one of the first true skyscrapers. How quaint and dated they looked now, but how ornate and proud they must have been at the time. He ambled past Giuseppe's Barber Shop, celebrating its 35th consecutive year in business. A favorite sign still hung in the window after all these years, "Appointments Not Always Necessary," above a drawing of a gentleman with shoulder-length hair above a wide collar and a healthy mustache. "Why Dad," he remembers asking at the time, "would anyone get their hair cut at a barbershop with a sign saying 'Appointments Not Always Necessary?'"

"You wouldn't, Francis, you wouldn't," his father answered, and smiled.

"Why then...?"

"Loyalty to Giuseppe," he quickly answered. "Wall Street was a tight-knit community in the '50s. Italian-Americans were not discriminated against, but they did have to work harder, and they kept to themselves. Italian delis and barbershops arose to cater to them. Giuseppe probably put up the sign to *try* to attract other clientele."

When his father said "back in the '50s," he made it sound like such a long time ago. Now Fran laughed quietly.

His father, though, grew wistful. "The '50s were the Golden Age. The era of men such as Victor Bergeron and Stanley Lieberman. Heroes of the Golden Age. I suppose you could say ethnicity was a challenge back then."

Afterwards, they would pile into the family car and roll back up to the early suburbs of metropolitan New York and converse over the tinny concept known as AM radio. He had a fondness for those pleasant car rides. A favorite pop melody of that era was on the tip of his tongue. What was that song?

Fran was too young to believe that America's golden age could have expired before he reached his teenage years, but as the country was at peace and the populace was in a hurry to develop, and the post-war psyche was underdeveloped, there was less occasion to undertake critical self-introspection and question the evolving but unplanned and invisible merit system that guided society's successes, failures and outcasts. As he aged and became more aware of the slight personality or chromosome flaws that could alter a person's behavior, and as he became increasingly frustrated with the tendency of governments to hoard resources, he began to realize that developing systems with few, but sensible and flexible rules was more equitable for ensuring that most people stayed on the correct side of the thin line and that society's resources were distributed equitably. A society in which outdated regulations outshine common sense is destined for stagnation, he realized, and little better than the twisted and selfish individual who cares not to tell the difference between right and wrong.

Moreover, as the early 1990s recession intensified, he was willing to stake a claim that any other era was gilded, as compared with the current.

This is not the occasion to elaborate more fully, but time permitting later, explain I will.

He continued walking, this time north and east until he reached the corner of South Street and Fulton Street. Wall Street had given way to the insurance district and then the early-morning fish market and thriving tourist area known as the Seaport. As Manhattan was running out of land mass, he reversed course and traversed west for a short while. He walked back and forth, staring at the ground, staring at the buildings, and staring at the sky. He walked south a block and did the same. And then another and another block. He leaned back against a stop sign and shook his head.

A few weeks earlier there had been a series of explosions. "The irony," he thought. "Explosions in the insurance district." He'd been tracking various "series of explosions" for the past months, throughout Europe and the Americas, on each occasion in the same style. Lots of property damage, lots of papers strewn from tall buildings, but never a human injury. The crimes were widely spaced. Months and thousands of miles apart. Had these actions required meticulous planning? Did the perpetrator take his time for effect, or was he a part-time bomber? Had the bomber now come home? he wondered.

He had all evening to reflect on these items; it was time to check in with his wife, for which he repaired to the nearest payphone. Unfortunately, a series of busy signals transpired before he gave up and decided to start asking questions.

He rounded the corner on which sat a tidy flower shop pun-named Dora's Plaice and walked into Hogan's, a white-collar bar with a blue-collar mentality, and by reputation some of the finest comfort food in the ZIP code.

Fran noticed his shoes scuffling lightly over the clean but aged tile floor as he walked to the bar and sat down next to a couple of young gentlemen. The tall, swivel-hip bar stools looked as uncomfortable as they did all the rage.

He ordered a draft from the bartender, put on his game face, and prepared to make small talk in a western New York accent.

"Hey, how ya guys doin'?" he asked. Did they wonder how corny he felt asking this question? However, his purpose was to sound neutral, in order that these two might volunteer something, a semi-conscious recollection, knowledge of physical evidence, any piece of useful evidence.

"Not bad," the gentleman closest to him said. "Considering." He paused, before continuing. "It's been a long day."

A long pause ensued, and Fran wondered whether this was a sign that these two were clammer-uppers. He took a gulp and started to sigh, until the other gentleman broke the ice.

"This is a little off the beaten track from the Seaport. What's a Midwestern tourist doing in *this* pub?"

"Oh, no...I'm from Syracuse, bud. I'm here on business. I, ah, work for a consumer products company. We just finished a long off-site conference and I decided I needed a beer. Our boss figured that Focus Groups are running into an Agnew Wall and he dispatched us to New York to cobble together a new way..."

"Agnew Wall?" the second gentleman asked after laughing good-heartedly.

"Ah," Fran continued, with relief. "It means you can fool some of the people all the time and all the people some of the time." His new friends nodded with approval, and laughed again. "You two must be locals, then?"

"Local to this area nine to five anyway," the first gentleman replied. "Not many people live around here. We both work in wholesale insurance."

Fran's eyes lit up, internally. "I'm sorry for you guys, in that case. I read about the explosions." Their eyes blanked. "Or do you work in a different part of the industry?"

"Like I said," the first gentleman repeated, a little coldly. "We work on the wholesale side. And the explosions occurred at night. No one at work. No injuries. It didn't affect us."

"Oh," Fran responded. "I'm relieved. So, what do you recommend to eat here? I'm starved."

"Everything's good," the second said. "Should we order a platter?"

"Platter—" Fran half-asked and half-stated.

"Uhm, yuh," he replied. "Fido back there calls it 'Wings, Rings and Other Things.' He says he's gonna copyright the name..."

"Fido?!"

"The bartender," who was plump. "Doesn't he look like he enjoys fried grease?"

Fran laughed through his nose. He raised a finger and affirmed, "I'm in." He pondered the idea of wings, rings and "other things." Though no one could top Fran's wings, this dish was pretty hard to mess up unless they were way under- or over-cooked. Fran would separate by section at the joint, wash and rinse in very cold water, steam for several minutes, allow to cool, coat in Mexican corn flour—fresh Mexican corn flour, *masa harina* to the Mexicans. What a scent! A universal peace aroma if such an item were possible—and hot paprika, onion salt and celery salt, bake until near done and then fry on medium-high heat for another 7-10 minutes, alternating a sprinkle of hot sauce, olive oil and a flip of the spatula. He used an extra-large, cast-iron skillet, because if you brown the wings too closely together they steam, rather than toast. He thought about the chili chocolate mango recipe that came with the skillet...Onion rings, though. Quite difficult for home cooks.

Blue cheese dressing. Near-ripe white Rouquefort cheese, buttermilk, fresh tarragon, celery and onion salt. Fresh lemon or lime juice, Spanish olive oil, hint of Tabasco, or Scotch bonnet. "Other things." Hmm...

The first gentleman noticed empty glasses and asked politely, "What you want to drink? What do you normally drink?"

"I travel a lot. I drink whatever local swill the bartender recommends, or whatever is on tap."

"This is gourmet grease. We needn't drink swill," the second gentleman cautioned. "Should we split a bottle of wine? What are you in the mood for..., I didn't catch your name?"

"Ah, Fran. Short for Frank or Francis. But, uh, my wife is the wine connoisseur. She chooses for the family."

"Another round of drafts then?" the second gentleman asked.

"Yeah," Fran replied hungrily and thirstily. "But let me call my wife and tell her where I am. The line was busy when I tried before. I'll be back in ten minutes. And if I'm not back when the food arrives, save me a wing."

Outside the heavy oak door, he watched as four young, professional women examined the menu, gazed closely through the smoked glass window, and debated whether to give it a try.

"It looks all right," one said unconvincingly. "Do you think there'd be a table for four?"

Fran offered his advice. "I would definitely. The food is excellent," he said, *very* convincingly.

"I'd need to find an ATM first," the ditherer explained.

Fran raised an index finger. "That...," he paused for effect, "I cannot help you with." He waited for the laughter of acknowledgment and then walked to his payphone.

"Dar, you're off the phone. How was your day?"

"Very busy. The day doesn't end when I get home. A doctor's day never ends when she has a beeper. Speaking of which, when will *you* be home?"

"Tough to tell, I'm making progress. There may have been witnesses."

Darby, or Dar for short, wasn't uninterested, but she was lost in thought and thus articulated a polite, "How so?" of acknowledgment, and shrugged audibly.

"One of the guys in a bar said 'It's been a long day' and then stopped. People don't do that in New York. They finish, or an associate finishes with, 'It's been a long week,' or 'It's been a long year.'"

"Did you tell them why you were asking questions?"

"No, I disguised my interest, just in case. I pretended to be an out-of-towner involved in consumer marketing. You never know who's listening."

"Okay, I need to go. I promised Mrs. Smith I'd call back. But I'm glad you reached me. Let me know if you'll be late."

Fran smiled by design. Darby referred to every mother whose name she couldn't immediately recall as Mrs. Smith.

He returned to the bar and resolved to ask the second gentleman questions avoided by the first.

"It was almost surreal," he admitted. "If you didn't work in one of the affected buildings, you could be totally unaware of what happened next door. No spillover, no structural damage. Amateur sleuthing became a cottage industry." He laughed at his joke. "These were insurance company buildings. The most popularly-held theory—probably still is—that the gang was out to destroy records. That's a laugh, though. Paper trails are computerized these days."

"If it was a gang," Fran offered.

The first gentleman bristled.

"My name's Fran, by the way," he said, to change the direction of the conversation. He forgot he'd already answered that question.

"We don't have names anymore," the second noted. "Meet Tweedledee," he pointed at himself, "and Tweedledum," as he pointed away.

"I take it you are the two who are inseparable?" Fran guessed.

Tweedledum smiled, slightly wryly. They saluted and toasted.

Fran excused himself to the men's room, where he madly scribbled as many notes as possible in a reasonable period of time. Being cautious, he recognized that were he to dawdle, a man with something to hide might become suspicious. He returned to the table, holding his stomach gently while sitting back down on the stool, visibly extracting a small package of Pepto-Bismol from an inner coat pocket.

"Everything come out all right?" the first gentleman asked.

"Yeah," he said. "Must be the Indian food I ate at lunch. We don't have *vindaloo* in Syracuse. Tex-Mex spices have no untoward affect on my belly, fortunately."

The bartender delivered the snack platter a few seconds later.

"And not a moment too soon!" Fran added comically. For those familiar with high school basketball practice procedures, imagine a smooth run-through of the three-man weave. For those not, simply imagine a feeding frenzy.

When the first gentleman had had a few bites, he lightened up a little. Perhaps his energy level was low, a conclusion Fran summarily drew.

"We actually did discuss the bombings, internally, quite a bit. It was pretty freaky, as you could imagine. It was like the opposite of a neutron bomb. But after the TV vans disappeared, media interest disappeared. I heard from friends and relatives also. They called the day after the explosions to see if I was all right, but a few days after a blast they would joke about it. The seriously sick jokes I didn't mind, ironically, because they were too absurd to be intentionally hurtful. But when they would say, 'At least it didn't happen in my backyard'..."

"Now we are all NIMBYists," his partner declared profoundly.

"NIMBY?" Fran asked with curiosity.

"Not in My Back Yard," he explained.

Shortly thereafter, the loud, haunting baritone of a young and intense songstress infiltrated Fran's head, as his head gently vibrated. He walked toward the back of the bar, which by then had become a dark, cavernous rock & roll arena. The melodies became louder and more haunting. Tweedledee and Tweedledum had deserted him. He walked into a speeding car, sat down in the middle of the back seat, decided he didn't like the driver's steering manner and opened the right side door, but the handle fell off.

His next sentiment was that of waking up startled, late the next morning. He jumped out of bed and checked his clothing, thrown messily over chairs. He was short a good deal of cash, but his other belongings were intact. No credit cards were missing, and his keys were on the credenza, where he habitually left them. In his back pocket was a small notebook; no pages missing, his Pepto-Bismol jottings intact.

In fact, aside from severe grogginess, a ringing headache, inconceivable recollections of the previous evening and unaccounted-for hours, nothing was missing.

He left the room and went into the kitchen. His wife stared at him, as if he were a fastidious man auditioning for the part of Pig Pen.

"You don't look like a man who's had ten hours sleep!" she observed.

"Anything unusual happen?" he asked, as if she were more likely to know than he.

"To who? To what?" she exclaimed.

"I don't know...to me?" he said with bewilderment.

"Couldn't tell you. You arrived after I went to sleep. You look normal, though you do have a ketchup stain on your collar," at which she pointed.

He felt the since-dried chili sauce stain. "My drink must have been spiked...hours are missing."

"Do you think one of the gang tried to poison you?" she asked.

"Potentially," he responded. "One of the witnesses *was* acting suspicious."

"Witnesses—" she stated.

"I have to think about this," he finished. "The explosions were well planned. I'm going to have to draw some diagrams."

Fran retired to the living room with a set of construction paper, an image of the globe lightly drawn in the background of each. He laid three on the dining room table and tossed the rest on the floor. He leafed through his notebook for a few minutes and began marking on the sheets.

He scratched his five o'clock shadow and marked circles around Montreal, New York, Cologne, Germany, Colon in Panama and Cuba, and Genoa, Italy. Below each he wrote the date and number of blasts, and where there had been multiple, the time span between the first and last. He repeated this practice on each sheet.

"Dar, something to tell you!" he yelled. She rushed in from the utility room.

"What is it, dear?" she asked with excitement.

"It couldn't have been either of the two at the bar. They can't be suspects after all," he recalled. "Americans can't travel to Cuba."

"What if they're part of a team?" she surmised.

"Not likely," he reposted. "Too far apart, not enough explosions in any individual city. Too specific. I'll tell you what, though. This is a man who wants his motive uncovered, even if he wants his own identity hidden." He paused for a few moments. "It's time to call Karl to let him know. I'll cook dinner once I'm off the phone and have had some more coffee."

Though Fran worked out of his home most of the time, he maintained a formal office in White Plains, the satellite city several miles north of Manhattan. In the early 1990s, White Plains was a tired city, with legacy department stores of faded brands, an overstretched commuter rail hub, traditional diners longing for their heyday, and morale problems in general.

Karl was his boss, and formerly his mentor. Unlike Fran, whose job was single-minded, Karl reported quite high up in the scheme of things, and constantly had the Assistant District Attorney for Southern New York breathing down his neck. It was perennially difficult for Karl to tell what motivated the ADA: getting crimes solved, playing political games or sucking up to his own superiors. Karl, for his part, shielded Fran and other subordinates from such nuisances, which allowed them to concentrate more directly on their narrower roles, but which also left Karl open to unjustified criticism.

Though another detective might have thought twice about calling his boss on a Saturday afternoon with generic information, Fran had no such misgivings.

"Karl, it's Fran. I'm making progress. The taxpayer's getting a return on his investment," he barked.

"Oh, Mr. Obrien," Karl's son, Cort, replied. "I'll just get my dad."

"Dad!" Fran heard Cort holler in the background. "It's Mr. Obrien!"

What a polite kid, Fran thought to himself. When Dar was comfortable enough in her practice, he'd like to raise a child that grew into such a presentable teenager.

Karl came to the phone. "Fran, it's Saturday afternoon. You are entitled to a day off."

"Thanks, boss," he teased. "Perhaps tomorrow. I thought while I had ideas fresh in my mind I'd give you a call. And after last night…"

"Why?" Karl asked, startled. "What'd I miss last night?"

"I had my drink badly spiked…" Fran started.

"Is that evidence? Have you requisitioned a fingerprinting?"

"No, I think it was someone who resented my disguise. I can't worry about that now. I'm getting to the bottom of the capers." He paused for effect. "Lucy Arnaz was right," he joked. "If you find the motive, you've found the motivation."

Fran knew what to say, but his head was still so frazzled he had trouble enunciating the words. "I'm on fumes. I'll explain everything in the office."

"*When* are we gonna see you in the office?" Karl pressed.

Fran thought for a moment. He needed to snoop around lower Manhattan once more.

"Probably Monday afternoon," he estimated.

But as we'll find out shortly, that forecast was to prove optimistic. It was not feasible to "snoop around" lower Manhattan with three oversized maps under his arms, and undertake a round trip from lower Manhattan to Millwood, mid-Westchester, to White Plains in one afternoon.

"Okay. See you then!"

The Feast

It was a tradition of Fran and Darby to mark the arrival of autumn and the end of winter with a grand feast, for which Fran held the pride of chefdom. On this occasion he decided to prepare a non-seasonal spread, incorporating several plates prepared ahead of time.

He whetted guest appetites with his middle-name appetizers of Drunken Cheese and Belgian Spears. The former consisted of goat's or semi-soft sheep's milk cheese, soaked in olive oil with olives, walnuts, pecans and garlic cloves, for at least 24 hours. The dunking vehicle was typically a chunk of *focaccia* or similar artisan bread.

The Spears were a combination of diced salad vegetables, hard Belgian or Dutch cheese, and chunky cold cuts evenly distributed on an endive or chicory leaf, held together by a toothpick. Though highest-quality ingredients were less essential for the Drunken Cheese—the slow blend of flavors of normally-immersible foods into the oil gave the appetizer its taste—for the Spear, quality was indispensable, because the palate would isolate a bland piece of cheese or an ordinary tomato like Russian cigarettes at a tobacco festival.

The main courses consisted of his variations of slow-cooked Moroccan lamb, *choucroute*, pumpkin and rice. Onto a saddle of lamb, Fran basted a mixture of pureed peas, diced onions, olive oil and spices, until the pea puree solidified into a golden-green crust on top, though with sufficient liquid in the bottom of the pan to allow for helpings of gravy. The spice mix was light and simple, incorporating cumin, paprika and sea salt.

Choucroute was among his favorite and simplest dishes, being comprised of layers of sauerkraut, sausage, bacon and meat hocks, trimmed of most fat. It was the herbs and spices which signified this dish—ground celery seed, onion salt, juniper berries, mustard powder, peppercorns and plenty of caraway seed. It was tough to tell whether it was the caraway that embellished the meat and fermented the cabbage, or the other way around.

"Green peppercorns are a luxury, but caraway seed is a *necessity*," Fran often whispered to himself.

But to others, the crowning glory involved the pumpkin: wild rice half-simmered with vegetable soup mix and chopped onion, oven-baked inside a fresh pumpkin. The rice-stuffed pumpkin was cooked first and left to cool, partly because of the astronomical temperature the rice reached inside the sealed vessel, but also because the oven was required for its brothers. Fran placed a medium and a large pumpkin in the hot oven, scrubbed on the outside but otherwise unprepared. When the medium pumpkin exploded, the large pumpkin was cooked to perfection.

Did I forget to mention the roasted garlic blue cheese ranch dressing? As classic as a clarinet solo in a Benny Goodman tune, how could I forget the blue cheese ranch dressing with roasted garlic?

When Fran was feeling octopus-handed, he would flourish by proxy, serving tapas-style meals to guests in split-level, three-inch diameter bowls. He would serve a simple glass of imported Argentine milk for desert. Diners would be doubly surprised, because Argentine milk tastes like a soda-fountain-era milkshake. Or on top of homemade ice cream he would sprinkle dehydrated Channel Islands milk, which is 25% creamier than normal milk. As a quick-witted advertising slogan-maker once noted, "The milk's so good the cows want it back."

On this feast day, though, Fran had energy enough only for an afterthought. He had a Carvel's chocolate ice cream cake delivered in the afternoon. "Everyone loves chocolate," he reasoned. "And I like Carvel's." Frank Carvel was another pioneer, both consumer and design, albeit in his own way, but he seemed to overlook—even reject—respect. Never mind, Fran thought, I like the ice cream.

Darby appreciated his eclecticism in the kitchen, equally because she was relieved he had a dedicated hobby that completely took his mind off work (when the risk arose that he could bore her, or others, with details of a particularly boring case, she could easily goad him into changing the subject and embarking on a fascinating or amusing tale of food discovery or a cooking experiment). Moreover, this hobby gently amused her in a way that few male hobby dedications truly could. "Who would imagine that 'The Belgian Spear' was the name for lettuce with chopped meat and other vegetables on top," she would laugh.

The beverage choice he left to Darby. In his view, it all boiled down to "house wine," though to the best of my knowledge, no one ever complained about her selections.

The normally verbose Fran was quiet this evening, perplexed by unsuccessful combination-running of bomber movements through his head. Unsuccessful in that he was unable to link the cities together by a common thread.

Fran excused himself early from Darby and their six guests, feeling exhausted but unaware of the toll the previous evening had taken on him. When he awoke after a night of deep sleep and intense dreaming, it was late Sunday morning. Fran and Darby enjoyed the sun's creeping warmth that day with long walks down the narrow, winding roads that so punctuate mid-Westchester County.

"How could a couple feel so at ease with each other after eight years of marriage?" Fran asked mid-way.

Darby paused, beamed, and reminded him, "We don't have children."

Fran smiled back, though not cognizant of the paradox of her words. He studied the lonely, depreciating snow bank by the side of the road. This was a bittersweet reminder that while another happy-bird-chirping spring beckoned, another season had passed without a resolution of the case.

Fear, Loathing and Exploded Pumpkins

Fran awoke at a normal hour on Monday and made his way downstairs for coffee, a little distracted but generally focused, until he pushed through the kitchen door. Standing in waiting, apparently for some time and with the oven door open, was their long-standing cleaning lady.

She pointed bluntly and informed him, "He who demeans it, cleans it."

"Oh,…mushrooms!" he cursed.

Fran exited Fulton Street Station just after rush hour and began to pace intently. Rather than scour the streets and buildings, he considered the informal lectures of his father and the many engaging, usually short, conversations with Karl's children.

How he longed to begin raising his own family. Until then, he had felt complete with his consuming job, hobbies and reading interests and, especially, his wife. But it was only when he contemplated again the words of his father that he realized what he presupposed was stream of consciousness—was wisdom. "How's a teenager to know?" he asked aloud. "Why don't teenage boys have curiosity?" What Fran never grasped was that his father had the inspiration to be a pioneer, but lacked motivation and pie in the sky, and also felt the time had expired for true modern American pioneers. Only of the Golden Age, though.

Fran reckoned there was not much he could accomplish in the insurance district that morning, and instead made his way to the New York Public Library, to conduct the research for which an obligation had been accumulating. To fit the pieces into the puzzle—or at least enough to be able to recognize the picture—he would have to understand the geography of the crimes. On a global diagram, they looked like a tidy constellation, as if the perpetrator was intending to draw one. It was increasingly evident that he desired his motive to be uncovered. The accelerating frequency of explosions in New York suggested, moreover, that he was ever-anxious for the riddle to be solved. The crimes were now centered in lower Manhattan, implying that it had become his base and he was going nowhere. It was merely a question of isolating the motivation, discovering the suspect, and sitting near the base until he appeared in public with incriminating materials.

Knowing the suspect's identity had finite urgency, as he was destined to strike again. Yet he was unlikely to be dangerous in the open air, as there was no suggestion he possessed firearms. So, while Fran was necessarily stressed about creating a short list of suspects, a blend of urgency and patience would serve him best.

In the Public Library, Fran studied the foreign cultures and languages of the countries in which the crimes had been committed, in furtherance of pinning down a link. He learned about the great waves of immigration that enveloped the northeastern part of the United States and Lower Canada, as it had been called, in the second half of the 19th century. He discovered, regarding his lineage, that at one point in the 1860s, as much as 25% of Boston's population consisted of first-generation Irish, predominantly from Cork. In the late 19th century, there were already as many as 30 recognizable languages spoken in New York City. According to one account, in the 1870s there were but five Hungarian families in New York, none of which spoke any other language. "Talk about language immersion," he said to himself.

He was particularly interested in the immigration patterns of Montreal, the site of small, seemingly unrelated explosions, until recently. These detonations had occurred much earlier, but now Fran was beginning to think they were tests, to see whether they could be conducted without causing human injury and without leaving a trail to the instigator. Just as a cleaner tests bleach on a hidden piece of fabric, to find the results of the test clean: examine the parts of the shirt that are normally tucked in. If, as Fran suspected, the seemingly-unrelated theory was accurate, he would soon be able to begin the tedious process of casting a net.

He stumbled upon a column of books about Spain's Sephardic heritage. Sephardic is the term which applies to Jewish people of Southern European and Northern African descent (Sephardic deriving from the Hebrew word for "Spain"), set against the Ashkanazics of Northern and Central Europe (Ashkanazic deriving from "German"). A by-product of the Spanish reign of terror in the 15th and 16th centuries was the near-destruction of the Sephardic culture, through annihilation and forced conversion. One of the great ironies of history is that the pre-Spanish-Inquisition era was perhaps the largest and most peaceful example of integration between Jewish and Muslim peoples. In the 12th century, 90% of the world's Jewish population was Sephardic, yet by the 20th century the percentage had fallen to 10%. The Sephardic culture thrived as never otherwise during the 9th to 11th centuries, yet Judaism in Southern Europe was now little more than a historical research topic.

Fran thought about a few of his other cases involving the Spanish. Despite the rocky politics of the recent and very distant past, Spain had nonetheless managed to attain a vibrant and admirable culture. Fran's mind began to revolve intently, he paused and then smiled poignantly. "Boy, does this guy HATE Columbus!" he shouted, to the consternation of individuals accustomed to library voices at the NYPL.

What then attracted Fran's interest was the stack of books describing the legendary cuisine. Of Spain's Jews, a tremendous combination of history, ingredients, fusion and experimentation produced an almost-perfect gastronomy. In the early 1990s, though, this was a largely unexplored subject. Excitedly, he gobbled up the books and recipes and imagined the feast in which a gourmet such as he could both prepare and partake:

Golden potato soup
Pumpkin pancakes
Meat loaf with sweet and sour tomato sauce
Meat-stuffed vegetables
Braised celery root and carrots
Pastry filled with almonds and honey and dipped in syrup

And finally, there was Cherry Pilau Chicken. According to the archivist named Marta, if you didn't like this dish, there was something wrong with you. Verily, this must be true, Fran thought to himself.

At this moment, Fran recalled his promise to show his face in the office, and he quickly called Karl from a nearby payphone to postpone his arrival by twenty hours. However, it wasn't Karl who answered the phone, or his lab assistant, Linda, but the intern, Andrea, who bore the awkward news that Karl's boss, the ADA, was shaking him down for results. "Make something happen!" he demanded.

Fran became nervous, because such arm-twisting from above can come to no good. It is natural that an ADA wants to be appraised of the status of an investigation, and as overseer of the office, this information essentially belongs to the ADA. However, the higher-up rarely asks questions for the right reasons, and even more rarely does the right thing with the answers; that is, keep them to himself unless he has something productive and measured to offer.

"Prepare the chart room," Fran announced. "I'll be there tomorrow morning. If we work together, we should be able to crack the first phase by noon."

Message to Garcia

Fran wasn't quite ready to present his ideas to Karl and Linda; they still needed a day plus of fleshing out. However, he'd been procrastinating for days and therefore concluded that loose thoughts were better than none, even if a complete picture was not much farther away. That presentation was overtaken by events, though, when the ADA unilaterally decided that Fran should track down the so-called Cuban Leads.

One of the blasts had occurred in the west central Cuban city of Colon, but due to travel restrictions placed on U.S. citizens, Fran was not able to fly there to investigate. Through a middleman, though, Karl was able to arrange a meeting with a Cuban witness, "Garcia," in a third country. Although inconvenient and expensive, Karl agreed to the ADA's request to send Fran to Mexico. According to the middleman, El Cubano was a talkative individual, and this would be an opportunity to quiz him on matters aside from the case at hand, which in Karl's view would mollify the ADA. Further, Karl explained, by talking up the value of the informant, he could effectively stall the inquisitiveness of the ADA. "Make sure you come back with something useful," Fran was reminded.

Fran felt the evidence already in hand was sufficient, yet he opted not to explain his misgivings about undertaking such a long journey with so little prospective benefit. There was no doubt, though, that he had personal reasons for accepting the trip. Fran had heard about the wonders of Cuban food, but most specifics had eluded him. However, there was no eluding the famous Cuban sandwich, which was plentiful throughout New York, or the café con leche. As a result, one of his conditions in traveling to Mexico was that the contact would bring a bag of the treasured Turquino Lavado coffee beans and a loaf of Cuban flatbread.

While en route, Fran reviewed in his mind one of his early and most complicated cases, that of a white-collar criminal who embezzled several million dollars from her employer, a money center bank. She understood the bank's front and back office systems so well she was able to siphon off approximately $100,000 per month without detection. The crimes went completely unnoticed for three years, until Fran's office received a series of calculated tip-offs on the QT. It took several additional months to connect the trail and apprehend the individual, during which the embezzlement dissipated and eventually stopped.

The suspect confessed to her actions when confronted and, with so much incriminating evidence and amid further substantiation that she acted alone, opted to plead guilty. Moreover, the suspect became a model prisoner in the white-collar jail, reading quietly and keeping to herself, apparently among the most serene the correctional facility had seen. The act of being caught precipitated her reformation, it seemed. Afterward, she became sought after for her "how did you do it?" input, first by the tabloid press and subsequently by data security and integrity departments of financial institutions. Before long, she turned this knowledge into a lucrative consulting business and she never, at least up to now, committed another crime.

Fran became curious, though, that there were tip-offs even while the crimes were otherwise undetectable, and that once the tip-offs commenced, the siphoning began to die down. Fran later checked the financial records of the bank and, to his surprise, discovered that the company's financial statements matched. Despite reporting losses, in footnotes to quarterly accounts, of course, no money had gone missing. She must have faked the crime because she felt that, as a young employee, her warnings about the poor security of the bank's firewalls would fall on deaf ears. Knowing this, she found it easy to create the appearance of a crime, and she was also responsible for the tip-offs. We were all taken in. Her ultimate goal was to build a financial integrity consulting business, but she felt that due to her inexperience at the time (and especially as a woman) no one would take her seriously. However, as a reformed white-collar criminal who had fooled one of the largest financial institutions in the world, she was now in a different league. In other words, the scam was the scam.

Fran raised this topic with the CFO of the bank, who gave an "arrest the usual suspects" response. Either the bank was aware of the double stunt and felt that publicizing it would do too much damage to its reputation, even at the cost of sending an innocent to jail—even an innocent who wanted to go to jail—or else he was so scornful of the individual that he just didn't care. Although not one of Fran's hypotheses, perhaps the CFO was, no more no less, a dope.

This was not the final punch line for Fran, though. To him, the conclusion was: it takes longer to catch someone who is acting alone. This case taught Fran a lot about personal and corporate psychology, and exceptions to the rule—as with D.B. Cooper and Robocop, the bad guy can be the good guy and vice versa—but also that banks carry plentiful reserve accounts to cover up errors.

The meeting with the informant was a bust. Not only did the Cuban not travel alone, but he resolutely clammed up during the meeting, contrary to the reputation which preceded him. Moreover, Mexico during 1992 was not the most user-friendly city to visit, even with the North American Free Trade Agreement about to start and the famous Mexican pre-election spending already underway.

These sentiments Fran readily shared from his hotel after the meeting, in the also-famous "New York no uncertain" terms.

"Karl, you promised this would be worthwhile!" Fran barked.

"Why, what went wrong?" Karl asked apprehensively.

"There were two of them," Fran explained. "Neither said a word. And they brought no damn coffee beans!"

"Two?!?" Karl questioned. "Garcia was supposed to travel alone. Did the contact offer anything?"

"Yeah," Fran said sarcastically, "a cigar, and as you know, I don't *smoke*."

"Neither spoke?" Karl asked disbelievingly.

"Yeah," he mouthed sarcastically. "When Garcia's attentive friend handed over the cigars, he said politely, '*Por favor*. We may be at war with you, but let's not go *overboard*.' No, they didn't say anything useful. But they asked many questions."

"Did you answer?" Karl asked inquisitively.

"Yeah, most of them, they were lay-up questions..."

"Why'd you...?"

"So sue me. They were easy."

"Didn't you realize the contact was possibly forcibly traveling with a spy?"

"I didn't tell him anything he couldn't have read in the *International Herald Tribune*," Fran replied. "There are no travel restrictions on Cubans to Mexico. That's why."

"They're gonna tell the spymaster we were cooperative."

"Even if the IHT...?"

"He'll be able to say his information is from notes taken in the meeting and we cooperated unknowingly. That the 'contact' gave us nothing. That they got one over..."

"Karl. Leave me out of your politics. The cold war is over. It's Cuba's 'special period in the time of peace.' They are harmless. And my *coffee*!"

"You don't realize how paranoid they are!"

"I'm not stooping to their level, or halfway, to yours."

"And what do you propose I give the ADA for our troubles and efforts?"

Fran thought for a moment and an idea clicked. "Cigars. Everyone loves Cuban cigars." Fran was right. In an ironic way, a southern New York ADA would love the gift of a Cuban cigar, illegal as these tiny things were in their own way.

"Yeah," Karl acknowledged. "Yeah, he will."

Tuesday Afternoon

Fran corralled Karl, Linda and Andrea into the situation room to debrief them on his findings. He had discarded scratch maps. and now on the large oval table was a fresh flat globe with deliberate markings. More important than the route map and travel estimates, though, was the research he had undertaken at the NYPL. In practice, the sheet was significant for the jumbo dots pinned on it, but little beyond that.

"Note the pattern," he began. "What's the common theme? There is no common thread. There were extraneous bombings; some carried out by our suspect, some not.

"He started in Montreal, where he's from, and finished, or is finishing, in New York, where he currently lives. Evidence from the first blasts threw us off, because they didn't have his 'fingerprint,' but in fact they were dry runs. The bookend blasts affected insurance companies, so we know he works in this industry. He's meticulous and cerebral, but not flawless.

"We had some trouble, some delays, because of poor translations, but...eliminate the bookends and the obviously unrelated attacks and we have cities such as Colon, Columbus, Cologne, Genoa, etc. Well, Colon is the Spanish name for Columbus, Spanish is the national language in most of his cities, and Genoa is the birthplace of Christopher Columbus. We were, admittedly, thrown off by Cologne, but that was his typographical error.

"The words 'colony' and 'colonialism' derive from the original Italian name for Columbus, so first I considered a grievance a bomber might have against colonialism. However, that black hole didn't mesh with Montreal. So I got to thinking, thinking a lot.

"To make a long story short, maybe he hates Columbus, but his primary point of vengeance is the glorification of the reign of Isabella and Ferdinand, and to publicize the great Sephardic culture these two destroyed.

"And the task ahead of us is simple, but painstaking—we need to check all the employees of the wholesale insurance industry in Montreal in 1990 and 1991, with those in New York City in 1991 and so far in

1992, with the commonality of a Sephardic name. If this doesn't work, we'll requisition airplane and hotel records, which could occupy us for months."

"Are you certain?" Karl asked.

"Yes, undoubtedly," Fran responded. "Victims of colonialism do not complain; rather, their champions, outspoken academics and actors, do. They have a different style. They are more verbally aggressive, but aren't violent—anymore. They file lawsuits," he finished with a smirk. Ten years later such fringe grievances would find homes on personal websites, but not in 1992.

Fran's conclusion was no doubt a hunch, and yet also the line of least resistance. It was not necessarily an inaccurate hunch, or that the line of least resistance wasn't the best place to start. With arguably no needles in the haystack of the Colonialism Theory, it was the only place to start.

"And the wasted time if your hunch is wrong?"

Fran didn't like the way Karl said "hunch," but he was too forward motivated to object. "We lose weeks at most. There's no logical explanation for the alternative hypotheses. Am I good to go?"

"GO!" Karl affirmed, and nodded his assent.

The Needle in the Haystack and the Damage Done

The search could have been performed in a variety of manners, but in attempting to best utilize resources, Karl, Fran and Linda agreed first to isolate last names common to Montreal and New York, and worry about the rest later. This was, in any event, desirable, due to the lack of specialized knowledge within Karl's unit.

Within a week, a list of about 1,000 names had been prepared and dropped on Fran's desk. A healthy Research & Investigation base, all in the office agreed. Given a steady pace and thick encyclopedia of Sephardic culture and names, Fran estimated that success—or not— would occur within another seven to ten days. However, before a few hours had passed, he came across a peculiar name—Lavi Leal Ladino— which was obviously not a birth name. Loosely translated, it meant "The Loyal Sephardic Lion."

"Tenspot!" he declared, nearly knocking over his coffee. Karl and Linda ran in.

"He *does* want to be discovered!" he cried. "Do we have home addresses?"

The Weekend Warriors

Fran held membership in a mid-Westchester club of former high school athletes who assembled on the first Saturday of each month to wear college "Property of..." sweatshirts and compete as aggressively as possible, yet in good faith—i.e., no dirty play. Depending on the season, it was flag football, in-the-grasp football (or fag football, as Dar jokingly called it), soccer, rugby league, street hockey, basketball, tag team cross country, softball the family event, and softball the drinking sport. Outdoor basketball consisted of five teams of five on five; the only difference from regular basketball being that a three-pointer was not a shot from beyond the arc (or "from Downtown" as announcers oxymoronically declare), but a swish from beyond 15 feet. "And one." It made total sense.

Lots of climates can beat mid-Westchester. Newport Beach most of the time, for example. But mid-Westchester the rest of the year has a tough time beating mid-Westchester on a near-warm sunny afternoon in late winter, especially when there are few other undercurrents of relative peace and calm.

The stakeout was due to start two days after the street hockey game. Moreover, these non-jock athletes had numerous subjects, many of them unpleasant, on their minds, this being late-winter 1992: recession, real estate crashes, sports league labor relations, etc. As a result, the first half was an excuse for several to exorcize their own private Idahos, and a rarified combination of pseudo-aggression, feckless cross-checks, and pre-nomenclature trash-talking followed. Rumble-like conditions did not persist, though.

Sports psychologists and talking heads are fond of declaring a peak-performing athlete to be in a zone. More relevant for these weekend warriors, and Fran in particular, was the runner's high that he achieved, in which the athlete plays silently in harmony with his teammates and achieves a quiet peace of mind. The Silverado Standard, one of Fran's teammates labeled it.

Fran's team finished a comfortable second, thanks in part to the runner's high, after which the moveable feast transferred to the town's small-C classic tavern, where the membership took turns holding court; that is, lecturing or facilitating discussion about a motivating topic. One of the gang of 25's unwritten rules - at least on the first Saturday of the month - was live and let live. One of the other rules was that minor transgressions were to be downplayed, especially through the third beer. However, the antics of one participant were so obnoxious they could not be overlooked. More irritating than his words was a pattern of extracting words from his mouth via hand gesture and expelling them toward the group via cliché. It had passed unnoticed to this loudmouth, then and since, that Fran was responsible for engineering an introduction to his spouse, on one wine-filled night, several years before. Fran, duly, had to bury him.

The boaster claimed there was no need to incarcerate white-collar criminals—if they're named and shamed, they won't commit a crime again. In other words, make 'em pay a fine and get on with it. Or put 'em under house arrest.

"First," Fran reminded him. "You assume everyone is basically honest. There are some who fundamentally can't tell the difference between right and wrong—violent or non-violent, it doesn't matter. Second, are you saying white-collar criminals are inherently better and more reformable, and shouldn't be subject to the same treatment under the law?" Fran was incensed. His livelihood was being belittled. "Why bother to catch them?" he asked rhetorically.

The dispute was over.

He also, though, found himself in temporary trouble when he nicknamed someone "Orange Blossom Honey." Being from San Francisco but not that way inclined, the recipient of Fran's nickname was likewise puzzled. "Don't take offense," Fran explained. "That's a culinary compliment. Have you ever tried orange blossom honey? It's amazing. Not only that, I have an English colleague I call 'Toasted BCM,' for Toasted Bacon, Cheese & Mushroom sandwich with Brown Sauce. Also simply amazing. England's culinary achievement. He doesn't mind the nickname, though he does insist that English chefs have more to offer... Remind me, next month I'll make a batch, um, make that half a batch of Toasted BCMs and half a batch of Cuban Sandwiches. Vanilla bean ice cream with orange blossom honey for dessert, or maybe just orange blossom honey with a spoon."

Fran was on a roll. The normally verbose Fran was verbose again. Without realizing, it had become his turn to hold court.

The offerings would prove as tasty as he maintained, even if no one else would be as focused on the process as he was. But he had other hurdles to clear first.

Squatter's Rights

It was 6:15 AM when Fran arrived at Fulton Street Station on the Lexington Avenue Line, anxious to examine the layout of the neighborhood for optimal waiting and resting places. The original stack of R&I files lacked home addresses, but Lavi Leal Ladino was indeed a one-of-a-kind name. Unlisted at that, but minimal string pulling was required to gain knowledge of the location. The apartment building was about half a mile from Fulton Street Station.

Fran came upon a merchant selling counterfeit goods from a vacant storefront that had been broken and entered. The peddler's van had moments earlier dropped off the day's merchandise to be recollected in the evening, lest another enterprising merchant sense an opportunity to intermediate stolen counterfeit goods. Wearing a face of authority, though no uniform or badge, Fran inspired a feeling of unease in the merchant.

He *could* write to the district chief about the illegal retail activity on this site, but it was an entirely different division altogether, and who knew whether the city law enforcement agencies would take any action, knowing another similar operation would merely open in its place the next day? The proper landlord was, in all likelihood, absentee—and possibly bankrupt. Fran's inquisitive glance, and the time of the morning, produced a derisive sneer from the merchant, even as Fran half-seriously considered sub-letting space at the back of the store. Fran glanced at the large, empty room lacking fittings and thought better of making a proposal.

"Squatters have rights, too!" the merchant sneered again. "We have a right to make a living."

Salt of the earth, Fran pondered briefly, and concluded it was better for this varmint to be selling fake goods in illegally occupied premises than to be conning tourists on the street or partaking in other forms of outright theft. But not by much.

He walked over to the Seaport and the wholesale fish market, trying to think of an excuse to buy a bushel of clams or a box of fresh cod. He gaped at the gigantic swordfish and tuna, having forgotten how large they grow. He examined each product as if he were the inventory manager at Mercado del Paz in Madrid, except with eyes of gusto. And how decadent: the daily toil of these workers was his quiet enjoyment. How pleasant an activity to observe.

"Squatter's rights," he whispered aloud. "Whatta concept. So do the crabs in this box." He looked down at a box of ignorant, crawling crabs on the wet floor and suddenly felt sympathy for them. "There ought to be a name for this double standard," he explained to the crabs, "in which the honest and hardworking are penalized for minor infractions, while education-shy rules-trespassers are given the benefit of the doubt." A lone crab was drawing too much attention to itself, and this was met by a playful spray from a power washer. "Oh yeah," Fran rippled. "That squeaky wheel got hosed."

In the background was the famous early morning café playing proud opera music, and posing as an attractive non-sequitur in this part of Manhattan. "A head or two of fresh, wet garlic could be quite a match for those Ipswich clams," he jotted mentally.

Nearby, a restaurant catering to the insurance district lunch crowd was opening its doors to employees preparing to chop their way into vegetable anonymity, and fry their way into the Southeastern Manhattan, potent-smell fish hall of fame. Power washers were the friend of fish restaurant owners everywhere.

What choreography in this part of Manhattan in the early hours, Fran reasoned. The rhythm and cadence of the fish market, wholesalers with names such as Monte's and Smitty's. Workers for whom the adjective "burly" was invented. The musical montage behind the snack bars, coffee shops and restaurants, and the light clack-clack of people walking to work. The regularity of the sounds. And no one getting in anyone else's way. During his post-case wind-down, Fran might return to this early morning scene and observe its calming effects without distraction.

Fran was now ready for the big event. The waiting, that is. Eventually Lavi Ladino would strike again. As Ladino was not aware he had been identified, he would take precautions no more vigilant than behaving discreetly. At the same time, neither Fran nor his men needed to take specific precautions, because there was no evidence that Ladino carried firearms and the risk of premature explosion, by action or inaction, seemed minimal. More to the point, Ladino seemed careful to exclude the possibility of personal harm. Despite his unusual motivation, he was not a danger, either to others or to himself. His modality seemed non-confrontational and non-violent, up until the point of attack, that is. Thus, as the suspect was being watched full time, the task upon Fran & Co. was merely to be patient, waiting for Ladino to bring the evidence out into the open, and that would be the end of that.

However, his plausible scenario was bluntly interrupted when the ADA insisted again that the authorities should "make something happen." Accordingly, the ADA sanctioned one of his offices to apprehend the suspect as soon as he was sighted leaving his apartment, and search those premises if necessary. It was late in the day that Karl and the ADA broke the news. Fran was discussing tactics with Linda when Karl invited him into his office.

"Fran," Karl started, "the ADA and I thought we should, as a matter of protocol, inform you of the decision to preemptively apprehend the suspect. It's been decided that we should send another team, with differing training."

Fran was decidedly perplexed. "'Differing training.' You know he's non-violent, right?"

"Oh, sure," the ADA responded. "But the units will be more prepared for contingencies, 'chase scenes,' and the like."

Fran was becoming incensed, as he didn't trust the ADA's preparedness.

"Well, it's your decision," he grumped. He turned toward Karl. "Does this mean I'm being taken off the case?"

"Not at all," the ADA replied. "The two groups are complementary."

"And merrily we roll along, is that it?" Fran snapped. He realized the decision was out of his hands—he had no vote in the decision—and reconsidered the ADA's refrain to "make something happen." Although his own plan was less aggressive, it was sound. And safe. Albeit more slow-acting.

Fran knew there was a chance the ADA's plan would backfire, though not in a manner he could have guessed. Coordination of the two groups would also pose complications. And then Fran nervously asked, "And you're aware he might not be so sloppy as to keep his equipment in his apartment?"

The ADA shot a glance which suggested he wasn't.

Fran continued, "He doesn't keep or leave anything, anywhere that would leave a trace. He's careful."

The ADA adopted an appearance of dumbness as Fran finished. "Do you think he leaves a copy of the front page of his lease on the door of every building he's blown through?"

Karl and the ADA then changed to expressions which indicated it was too late to turn back. Fran departed.

As soon as he was out the door, the ADA closed it and explained to Karl, "You gotta fight fire with fire, and I just don't think Fran is fire."

Fran didn't need an insult to be motivated to stand up for himself. Just the same, he didn't need help standing up for himself. Moreover, the ADA needn't have shut the door, as this was not an occasion for taking crap, and Fran was out of the office before the ADA had uttered his first incongruous cliché.

Fran arrived home in a huff, and didn't settle down until dinner was half-finished. He almost didn't want to discuss with Darby a technique he visualized for baking shrimp in a rectangular cake pan to make the dish taste fried without the sense of greasiness, or the miraculous effect of placing an orange slice in Mexican beer, as opposed to the pointless marketing ploy of a lemon wedge. His stream of consciousness continued.

"Someone told me it's more effective to foam milk in a toddler's 'sippy cup' than with an expensive Italian espresso machine. Do you have any spare sippy cups at your office?"

Darby cracked up, if only because this was a perfect inadvertent statement, at exactly the right time. Until then, the viscous tension and Fran's silence was driving chills up her spine. She now wanted to drive to CVS immediately and purchase a Tigger sippy cup and a bottle of milk to watch him make this "better than Milano" cappuccino with toddler props.

However, conditions shifted for the worse shortly thereafter when the phone rang, with Karl on the line. He rarely called in the evening, which alerted Fran and Darby immediately to the likelihood of bad news.

Karl was agitated on the phone. "Fran, they went in!"

"Went in? Who? Already?"

"There's a lot more. They followed a young man meeting the description..."

"Description?"

"The ADA's men called the Personnel Department at the suspect's firm. Claimed it was a routine police—"

"What!?"

"They followed the man on a cycle."

"Cycle? He doesn't have a bicycle! I may be annoyed with the ADA, but I would have told him the guy doesn't ride a bicycle, if he'd asked."

"Uh, that's not all." There was a long pause. "He was knocked over! One of the ADA's men chased him and he sped up, and then around a corner, and was knocked over by a truck."

"Oh, my…is he…?"

"The officers assumed an innocent civilian wouldn't cycle evasively. When they picked up the body and felt no pulse, they phoned the ADA, who called an impromptu press conference to declare matters resolved. But it was cancelled just as abruptly when an officer checked the cyclist's wallet and noticed non-matching names. However, the ADA thinks he has this covered; that he can add a murder charge on the grounds of provocation and circumstances."

"That greedy twerp!" Fran began to rage out of control. "I'm blowing the whistle on him!" Fran hung up. He lifted the phone out of its module and heaved it against the wall.

Not in the right order, he paused, then counted to ten.

"Dar!" he shouted. "We're going to need a new phone." He paused. "The wall should be okay, though."

Although he was still irate and the camel's back of vengeance had borne one too many straws, he knew that whistle-blowings against ADAs do not come without consequences.

He called Karl at home on the spare phone, apologized to his son for calling so late, and felt slightly guilty when informed that Karl was still at the office and having to burn the midnight oil—important and competent decisions having been taken out of his hands, too.

Fran called the office and spoke to Karl in a calmer voice this time. "Tell the greedy twerp that I'll be cleaning up his mess within the next 24 hours."

"Delivery for Mr. Ladino"

Though Fran had seen the suspect walking in and out of his building a few times, he had only a vague idea of his schedule. As a result, he thought it best to arrive early, before Lavi had left for work. If the suspect was an earlier worm than Fran had planned on, he would arrive 15 minutes earlier the next day, and so on, as necessary.

Fran disembarked at Fulham Street Station at about 7:15 AM and began a deliberate walk toward the suspect's street. Perhaps tomorrow I'll celebrate my day off by repeating these steps and experiencing this part of Manhattan with a weightless mind, Fran imagined, without visualizing that it could happen. He crossed Water Street and bought two coffees to go from Das Opernhaus Café.

Until then, his mind had been filled with aggressive chatter, but as he re-crossed Water Street, he passed a street musician playing an accurate version of Boss Man of Bow Castle's axiomatic song, "Sweetness." Fran began to hum the backing vocals ardently. He withdrew a five-buck bill from his pocket and dropped it in the musician's top hat.

He walked by a school and overheard young students playing outside. There is nothing quite as joyous as the sound of children at recess, he reasoned. "Enjoy it while you can, kids!" he mouthed rhetorically in their direction.

Fran hummed to himself the opening instrumental verse to "Sweetness," loving the musical rhythm and the phrase, "Sweetness of the dawn; sweetness in your eyes," without realizing that the remaining lyrics spoke of hopeless desperation. Just like Lavi.

Fran approached the building's superintendent and explained that the suspect may have witnessed the previous evening's bicycle casualty, which had been intermittently reported on the local news. The two of them walked up the stairs to Lavi's apartment, by which time it was 7:45 AM. The super knocked on the door and yelled that other dwellers on this floor had reported problems with the hot water, and did Lavi mind if the super came in for a few moments to check that his apartment did not have the same issues?

The suspect opened the door innocently and was shocked to see

Fran standing with the super, but was unsure why. His favor done, the super walked downstairs inefficiently, unaware of the notoriety that his building would soon embrace.

"The man behind the curtain I presume?" Fran asked, almost with relief that the ordeal was coming to an end. "Fran Obrien. Nice to meet you. The super let me into the building."

Lavi, nearly dressed and wearing a visage which said, "Ten more minutes and he would have missed me," looked like a Canadian-Spanish composite, a dark-haired man who would not have been out of place anywhere in Europe or North America.

"I bought an extra coffee if you'd like one. A bit too early for Cherry Chicken Pilau," Fran noted. "The coffee is from Hogan's."

Lavi's change of expression indicated a clear lack of comprehension, which implied that it wasn't Lavi who had spiked his drink. Although irrelevant to the case, Fran needed to know.

And then it hit Lavi why Fran was there. If he could have fainted, he would have. He sat down on the nearest chair. After Lavi composed himself, he said, "Thanks for the coffee. Do you mind if I call my boss to tell him I might be a bit late?"

When Fran returned an expression that even Tennessee Tuxedo's stable mate knew meant "that won't be necessary, he already knows," Lavi slumped further in his chair. A few moments later, Lavi offered, "So no big deal, eh? You found who you were looking for."

"No big deal?!" Fran fumed. "I've wasted 18 months of my life on you!"

"I started only 16 months ago..." Lavi began.

"Whatever!" Fran exclaimed. "I've chased you half-way around the world!"

"You're well-studied...you caught me without making a splash," Lavi said, as a backhanded compliment. "You'll know I'm right."

"What? You've committed crimes," Fran continued.

"Columbus," Lavi indicated. "This Columbus Day bullshit. Columbus was financed by blood money from the biggest mass murderer of the first half of the Millennium.

Fran's retorts were ready, but he decided to let Lavi continue.

"After the Holocaust, the world said 'never again,' but this same world is oblivious to the real 1492. Forced exiles and conversions, murders, destroyed heritage. All that, and more. Isabella and Ferdinand forged and institutionalized religious persecution," he said with confidence and conviction. "If the world had stood up to them back then, there would never have been a Holocaust. There would not be today's level of tension between Jews and Muslims. I can't explain to you the amount of unnecessary aggro I endured from siblings of my Arab friends growing up in Montreal."

"No," Fran explained. "Isabella did not pioneer religious persecution." Fran was bemused that Lavi's historical knowledge went back 500 years, until which it was sound, but that there it stopped. "I think you'll find that it's the English you hate, not the Spanish."

Lavi looked puzzled. Fran continued, "King Edward's Expulsion Order of 1290. In the 13th century, public feeling against the Jewish population was running high, because of a very few unscrupulous money changers. The king, though, eagerly tolerated the prominent Jewish bankers, because they helped arrange financing for his wars, and because of the high levies he charged them. He *had* to borrow from the Jews, because at that time it was illegal for Christian bankers to charge interest. However, these taxes eventually drove the bankers out of business, and when this source of tax revenue dried up, the entire Jewish population became a liability for him. King Edward had the choice of permitting gangs of marauders to terrorize this group of innocent civilians or exclude it from the English nation altogether."

Fran paused and continued. "Four years after receiving a letter via the Archbishop of Canterbury, warning about the pernicious consequences of Jewish religious study, Edward I issued a royal decree, giving Jews three and a half months to leave the country or face execution. If you have a vengeance, that's it," Fran finished.

Lavi was speechless.

"Listen," Fran continued. "I have no love for the English myself. I'm half Irish."

"So why don't *you...*?" Lavi asked.

"Because it was centuries ago," Fran reasoned. "'Don't forget, but forgive those not responsible.' And get a life."

"What's your other half?" Lavi asked curiously, in a way that expressed vague familiarity, rather than their obvious adversarial relationship.

"Hungarian," Fran replied matter-of-factly. This was met by a blank, crumpled stare from Lavi. "There's no one the Irish didn't marry," Fran explained dryly.

"Hungarian?" Lavi questioned, expressing slight disbelief. "Why do you have an Irish first name?"

"Yeah, right!" Fran retorted. "Like I would have survived junior high during the Cold War with a name like Balázs."

Faced with a case of mistaken identity, Lavi wondered whether he would be able to escape from Fran's grip and instigate the type of commotion and mayhem among the British royalty and aristocracy that would draw attention to this mistreatment, but realized it was hopeless. "Well, it doesn't matter. No one was hurt."

Lavi then acknowledged an obligation to reply to the "you can't be serious" expression on Fran's face.

"The insurance companies have it all covered. Everything is replaced at no cost to the property owner. Even the insurance companies are reinsured; the costs are so widely dispersed that no company feels anything significant. It's not even a blip to the shareholders. Not only that—a few of the large insurance companies collude and wildly overcharge their customers. We who work on the inside know how scandalous the conduct is."

"Lavi, you've committed crimes. There are consequences. If you have evidence of illegal corporate activities, you could have documented it and sent this to the ADA's office. I know you're sharp enough to have grasped that." Fran thought for a moment. "It's not too late. If you can provide evidence, the authorities might take this into consideration."

Fran had had enough. It was time to end this saga. Though Fran had an appreciation for Lavi's circumspection and mental diligence, he found the self-righteousness irritating. If Lavi wanted to help himself, he knew how. Fran did not mention the potential murder provocation charge, but didn't deem this a realistic accusation in the final analysis. He led Lavi down the stairs, where a vehicle was awaiting them both. Before leaving, Fran looked around the front room of Lavi's apartment. It was completely normal.

The Ends, the Means, and That Which Lies Between

Fran and Darby were sitting at the dinner table discussing the end of his case, the distinction between purpose and methods, and the inability of certain humans to distinguish between the two. Sixteen months of his life had been single-handedly devoted to tracking down an elusive but determined bomber. In the end, justice was served, more or less, in Fran's view.

Had this been the best way for Lavi to propagate his cause? Perhaps as a loner, it was. Though media attention had been plentiful, and though the attacks were linked by identical signatures, Lavi thought the world at large would be clever enough to solve his riddle—which it wasn't—and therefore his cause itself was underreported. As the 500th anniversary of Columbus's landing on Hispaniola approached, the local press would focus more intensely on the towns named after Columbus (and Cologne mistakenly) and the common link of the bombings did prompt resident introspection and media dissection of whether they should be proud of their namesake. Do the ends justify the means? Can you just say Fuck-It! and grab the ends?

But that was then. That was then.

Fran and Darby were enjoying the aroma of the Nuevo Leon Chicken in the oven—chicken marinated overnight in fresh orange juice, chopped wet garlic, celery salt and habanero chili peppers—and blue corn and bacon cornbread, with orange blossom honey waiting for dessert. They were about to start munching on a Belgian Spear filled with honey-barbecue smoked salmon, vine-ripened high-pH tomatoes, manchego and homemade mustard. A wine of Darby's selection was sitting between them.

"Tomorrow morning," Fran started, "I'm going to South Street to watch the early morning symphony. I promised myself I would, once the case was closed and the loose ends tied up. I won't blow the whistle against the ADA, because I think he knows that if he manufactures charges—"

Darby interrupted. "You've talked about it so much, I feel like I know the Seaport without ever having been there. Can I come?"

Fran thought she was joking, so he laughed. She didn't laugh, though. "You're serious?"

She nodded.

"We'll have to be out of the house by six," he cautioned. "We have to stay out of their way; these are men for whom the adjective 'burly' was invented. And you have to listen carefully for the opera music, with all the surrounding noise. The Seaport that early is an acquired taste. It took me a month."

She nodded again. "I do have tomorrow off."

"You will love it," he encouraged. "The people who work there are *so* endearing."

"And we can talk about what I want to do next," she noted. "When I feel tenured at the practice, I won't have to drive myself so hard."

Fran knew exactly what she meant. He grinned even more broadly. He developed goose bumps all over for his wife and their just-agreed-on first child.

They were speechless for several moments.

Fran then began to dry swallow, and after about ten seconds, asked Darby rhetorically, "What if Lavi was right?"

The remainder of "Sweetness" played disturbingly in the background.

THE SLAM BOOK

"When the beat brings a beer, it's hard to get parted."
Lisa Buell

The Rap Battle

Johnny decided to revive the genre after he observed, at a semi-urban shopping mall, rap artists slamming each other in a contest format, "battling" as it's known in the malls. What appeared to be blaring DJs practicing for onlookers was actually a winner-take-all match. The observers were paying customers, the losing contestant having to cough up his own money as well as pride. Naturally, each battler brought his own boom box and cheering section.

Today's challenge pitched Don, tall and impressed with his looks, against Chino, slightly below-average in size and of very mixed race.

This is how it went:

"Little man, don't have no plan,
Can't stand up to Don, your beauty's non,
Don't have yellow skin, don't have hair that's thin. You don't fit in,
So you say you're black,
No way yo attack Big Don and my loyal pack."

Polite applause followed, mostly from Don's section. The crowd was clearly there for the underdog Chino, an outsider by skin color and neighborhood, but also fearless and already building a reputation as a battler. As it turned out, extra effort was surplus to the purpose of besting Don's mild insults.

Chino turned on his box, pumped his arms a few times and began:

"Got no need for a lengthy spiel when that's what passes for you keepin'
it real.

Hey there Jake, why you always on the make?
If some humility you would take, maybe you could use your snake!"

Chino won hands-down. He was the new champion of the Queenstown Mall. This wide section of the atrium would be his throne every Tuesday afternoon until he was out-battled. Don walked away frustrated and Johnny walked away fascinated.

Johnny

Johnny couldn't sing.
He couldn't rhyme, much.
And he couldn't spell, the first time anyway.
He was overly sensitive.
But he had an untapped flair.

Johnny's roommate in the small, two-bedroom Queens apartment was Happy Hair, a coworker at the plant, and the source of many of their mutual friends, but from the scientific rather than the engineering ranks.

The other prince in this triumvirate was Mano, himself the product of a flawed identity. Because he gestured with gusto, bobbed his head whenever he heard music, loved to belly butt and was believed to be Italian-American, Happy Hair and Johnny nicknamed him *mano a mano,* mistakenly believing this was Italian for "man to man." Mano, not being Italian, wouldn't have known that either.

For a long time, Johnny failed to grasp concepts such as status or position. He often felt inwardly awkward. I don't know why. There was no clear reason. Sometimes these things just happen. Johnny was challenged in other ways. He was mildly dyslexic, occasionally inarticulate, and formerly asthmatic, meaning he could be found short of breath or deep breathing.

Feeling vulnerable, he would let himself feel intimidated, either because he couldn't read another individual's personal makeup—or didn't think to try. To his credit, he declined to gossip and steered clear of the faulty-first-impression pattern. To his detriment, though, he failed to gain the beneficial feedback that can be derived from sharing personal information.

And he was prone to sporadic outbursts, when a member of the public crossed a line from normal to irritating, or performed one of Johnny's pet peeves. There's a fine line between justifiable criticism and whining, but there's also a thick line between complaining and letting it go.

There will be plenty of time for it to unfold whether any of this will come back to taunt him. Moreover, this is not the occasion for over-psychoanalyzing Johnny, or for listing his mild foibles. Lest we be derailed, all books were reopened after he witnessed the rap battle.

While on the bus back to his apartment, Johnny gave the event more deliberation. Though he was awed, this was not poetry. It was an encounter of quick-witted, rhyming put-downs. Were Don and Chino intending to be poets? He didn't think so. If so, that would stain the impression.

Johnny didn't appreciate modern poetry, either. It rhymed and was tedious or didn't and was tedious. These sentiments he could explain fluidly. Imagine a poem that conforms to the formula of post-1950 requirements, yet is rejected by those "in the know" because it lacks contemporary nuances.

Though he wasn't fond of other forms of verbal manifestation—he found classic poetry too profound and popular music catchy at best—this reflected his awareness that something was missing. He felt strongly about the topic. What did this novice understand that others didn't, and what was missing?

In contrast with other subjects, he didn't criticize composers because of a petulant dislike or lack of comprehension. Rather, he was trying to understand his own arrangements and style better.

Johnny had no vocational proclivity toward poetry, or relevant training, merely an ability to express himself in short bursts. Perhaps with musical education, or if he was more well-read, he'd have found career potential in verse. As a mechanical engineer, he was about average, skilled enough for respectable performance reviews, but not for the predestined fast track in engineering or management. About five years after he joined the pen manufacturer, that began to change. Johnny came out of his shell and his foibles dissipated, or anyhow became less visible. He had Don, Chino and their possés to thank.

Return to the Planet of the Eights

As far back as junior high, Johnny and other friends composed underground magazines they called Slam Books, a hobby which for Johnny continued into adulthood. The idea of the slam book was to personalize your life on paper, with stories, drawings, captions, lists, etc. The drawings need not be convincing, as long as they were consistent and recurring. Friends, enemies, rivals, role models, teachers, adult figures, and so on.

It was apt that Johnny's modern slam book would be labeled *The Pengineer*. Though it was a sideline, a distraction from the intensity of mechanical engineering, written to amuse himself, to blow off steam, Happy Hair encouraged Johnny to photocopy and distribute *The Pengineer*, foreseeing it would gain a quiet following.

This he did through posters in the cafeteria and eventually word of mouth. Internal policy forbade that he should charge a subscription fee, or that he labor on it during company time. Still, his boss, Mr. Benton, encouraged him, believing it would raise morale. And Johnny wasn't malicious. (Much, of course.)

Senior management loved the magazine and was relieved at its inoffensiveness, even when he sarcastically founded the white-collar trade union General Representation of Industrial Pen Engineers, or GRIPE.

He invented a puzzle game he named Zipswitch, whose only objective and attribute seemed to be that every other edition it was compelling and addictive.

However, he did foster arguments. For example, when it was the birthday of an old friend who had died prematurely and he compiled a tribute called, "Doesn't anyone have friends who have died of AIDS anymore?" For some, this tribute backfired no sooner than the title.

And his least-favorite bands. Well, how could anyone like Earth, Wind & Fire? But some people like Billy Joel, the Bay City Rollers, the Eurythmics. It made him want to confide to the girlfriend of the man who selects one of these artists on the jukebox: "Come back disco, all is forgiven!"

In sum, it was about caricatures, nettles, rants, raves, amusing topical events, and a small amount of poetry. Where the former was deadpan, the latter had style and emotion; while folks at work connected with the former, he connected with the latter.

Johnny's curiosity about poetry proper gradually accelerated. If "poetry battles" didn't exist, there was an untapped market opening, he reasoned. In fact, they did exist, but this being poetry proper, they were coincidentally called "slams," also, rather than "battles." It would be a little while longer before Johnny would discover this, though not much longer still before he worked up the courage to perform at one of them.

In the meantime, he passed his time designing and testing pens, writing (thesaurus in hand) *The Pengineer*, hanging out with Happy Hair and Mano, and accumulating acquaintances as a by-product of these three. Exchanges with these social contacts detracted from his restlessness. Without the sensation of a fix which came from what he called an "agreeable interaction"—he never said these words out loud because he knew they sounded pompous—he became, plainly put, insecure and unsettled. He blamed himself if he caught someone at the wrong time, moody, or if a conversation ended on a bad tone.

He was close to his family, but being in his late-20s and not well-traveled, he considered central New York State distant. Most, Johnny and his mirror included, considered him an ordinary engineer with run of the mill looks and personality. As he had been writing slam books for fifteen years, Johnny downplayed the initiative and imagination required to produce *The Pengineer*. Meanwhile, several circles of friends evolved, some closer and smaller than others, and they did not intersect. To some of Johnny's acquaintances, therefore, it was curious that he didn't seem to have many friends outside the circle they were aware of, but he didn't know how to make the circles cross.

Oh yes, you were probably wondering what it looks like:

The Pengineer: Issue #3

Friday Afternoon Quarterback: Now We Are All Pengineers

We will no longer be disconnected from our product. We will no longer produce a mass-market, inanimate object pretending merely that we offer "a superior writing experience" as compared with our competitors. We will use the product. It doesn't matter if you are unpracticed, inarticulate or have no sense of humor—and Lord knows some of you try too hard—as long as you try. Now, to the rest of you; come on in, the water's fine, but two notes of caution: do not be camp or excessively profound: Chuck Barris will gong you every time you attempt a Renaissance Europe impersonation or accent. And please, please do not be judgmental! And with that...

Think yourself alive!

The Water Cooler Absurdity

The company's senior elk, in their infinite wisdom, have declared it acceptable to drink water at our cubicles, but not coffee. Because water coolers and cups are provided, mugs have been banned. However, the cups are conical, implying there is no place to set them on our desk. I therefore challenge the firm to provide large conical cups—if that is its preferred shape—and in-built cup holders, for all employees so requesting—or, better yet, a coffee cooler.

The Poetry Burn—Paraphrasing Shakespeare

It is a wonder that we survive, with a CEO who art a mountain of mad flesh, though the best o' bull's pizzle cut-throats. When I read the annual report, I concluded thou sham'st the music of sweet news. Moreover, as Hamlet said, thou assume a virtue if you have it not. I believe thy sin's not accidental. And his wife appeareth nothing to me but a foul and pestilent congregation of vapours. Such a fustilarian! My boss will tickle your catastrophe, for you are as rheumatic as two dry toasts!

The Character I Love

There is a man on my bus, in a three-piece suit with short, bouffed hair perfectly in place, and perfectly behaved son and daughter, nearly every morning. What bravery to appear in public like this in the 1990s, and what lack of superciliousness for children to behave so well without an ulterior motive.

Readers: help me with a name! I'm visualizing every jacket thread and hair neatly in place—he looks like a *New Yorker* cartoon—but I cannot conjecture a suitable nickname.

The Poetry Slam

The lack of adverse reaction to Issue #3 was all Johnny needed to sign up for the microphone. Nonetheless, it was brave to speak at his maiden slam without the experience of attending as a spectator. He felt the Queenstown Mall battles were close enough.

At about 7:00 PM on the particular Thursday, Happy Hair's college friend, Rachel, buzzed the apartment bell in accordance with an arrangement to attend the event together. While Johnny and Rachel stood in the living room awkwardly, waiting for Happy Hair to finish prepping, Rachel eyed a sheet of half-legible scribbling, which read as follows:

> *"As compromising as the situation was, better to forget the dialogue clouds in your mind. Better to apologize and move on. Better to speak your piece, find your peace, and stop dwelling. Better to do your best and then relax. And live."*

"Johnny," Rachel asked. "Did you write this?"

From the tone of her voice, it was clear to us she saw Johnny in a different light; a man of sensitivity, vulnerability, thoughtfulness, emotion, not a soon-to-be go-for-it amateur poet. More than he saw himself.

"Yeah," he replied. "Practice sheets." He paid no other attention to her words or the expression in her eyes. "Happy Hair takes so long to get ready he could be a teenage girl."

Rachel wondered whether to follow up on either, but instead opted for the middle ground. "I'm looking forward to your reading. Are you going to give it your best shot?"

"Oh, no," he laughed assertively. "I would be too nervous. I'm going to play it safe. I've memorized a few paragraphs and have a few note cards in reserve..." His voice tailed off. "We'll have to see what the crowd mood is like."

Inspiration from the Band Shell

As Johnny, Happy Hair and Rachel walked to the slam, two 19-year-olds were improvising moves in front of a band shell, seemingly for the benefit of a blaster playing music which suited their choreography flawlessly. Johnny's eyes were fixed on the girls as they walked past and wanted to stop, watch and ask questions, but he fretted it would be clumsy all around, and thus denied himself the moment. Though a production in a ballroom, with a larger troupe, would lack the spontaneity and space afforded in the open air of this park, he nonetheless regretted not ascertaining whether these steps were part of a formal performance. He abhorred his natural reticence and the implicit color barrier that still existed in New York. The girls, with a fascinating combination of dance, music and surroundings, wouldn't have bitten. Indeed, they likely would have approved of public admiration. "Maybe Chino knows them," he speculated, and wrote off the opportunity. Why he didn't return another day with a borrowed camcorder, I don't know. Then again, little did *he* know.

The Poem

The slam took place in the back room of a Queens bar. They arrived as novices, like an adult caught off-guard by a cell phone's unusual ring tone. Confusion prevailed initially at the lack of entry fee. It did make sense, though, because the sponsor understood that a full back room meant ample beverage sales. The organizer knew his target market.

A wide variety of styles and verbosities unfolded; from the serious to the too-serious, from the humorous to the too-ironic. Poets speaking in a certain style to appear hip, or faux-angrily lecturing about political topics. Refreshingly absent were cover versions of poems one pretends to appreciate because the author is famous.

However, there was no one who could propel a phrase as could Johnny. He was nervous beforehand, in this crowded small room. It was rational that he feared both the unknown and familiar, with friends in attendance, *and* this was his first public address. *The Pengineer* was brash and controversial, but few of its loyal readers knew his face. He was both well-known and anonymous.

As a result, behind the lectern he was mentally serene but physically jittery. His knees were locked from tension and his fingers were clenched and taut. Though he memorized breathing and relaxation exercises, now was not the time to remember them. He smiled when he recalled the counsel of hefty Barry, head of the cafeteria, upon hearing Johnny's predicament. "The standard procedure is to picture everyone in the audience naked," he had explained.

"The standard response to that advice is, 'not if they look like you, I won't,'" Johnny had retorted. Barry's intervention was banal but effective.

And then Johnny recalled vividly the scene of the band shell dancers and the soothing vocals from their overextended blaster. The last of the tension parted.

> *"Roll the window down, if you dare,*
> *Dragon-blind wind sails through your hair,*
> *Emotions tamed and fair, passions consumed*
> *everywhere,*
> *Scent of dried leaves burning in the air,*
> *If you know what I mean,*
> *If you know what I mean,*
> *Still, who can envision behind this glare?"*

His pace quickened:

> *"When I was young I had a dream,*
> *Of a sheltered meadow by a stream,*
> *Of angels trapped and feelings doomed,*
> *Frowning children, drowning teens,*
> *A gesture made, the angels freed,*
> *The peril spent, the illusion flee'd.*
> *Ever since, since I was sprite,*
> *It has been my guiding light,*
> *That every tunnel has a light."*

He paused.

"What the fuck, it rhymes."

He stopped, and exhaled. The crowd paused and he continued.

*"I was chairman of the bored, I was bored of the
rings,
So I started writing slam books, to stir up some
things,
I slurred my boss's bosses, even though they're
kings.
What was I thinking, creating an inferno?
What was I doing, sticking my head in Sterno?
They read my rags, nodded 'why not?', even praised
'em now and then—
Or was it: as and when?
How did I survive this, with eight out of ten?
The bosses loved the satire, of, the jester makin'
pens!"*

He smiled and lowered his head slightly. He was finished.

The crowd erupted.
Imagine if he'd known how to work a crowd.

The Pengineer: Issue #11

Three months later, he reckoned the readership was well enough established to publish a pretend interview with the *Village Voice* and a local TV channel.

The Interview

In the style of a square, skewed Dylan—or Beatles—interviewer during the 1960s: "So, Mr. Johnny, who would you say were your greatest influences?"

"Oh, Dean and Cathy Moriarty, without a doubt," I told 'em.

The Beatles interviewer asked what got me interested in magazine publishing: "Was it the Internet chat room craze?"

"No," I immediately responded, though without the scorn I felt internally. "It was a fad in my central New York State town. I've been writing Slam Books since I was a young teen. Only for me this fad continued."

I longed to be asked the irrelevant questions that reporters ask celebrities, as if a celebrity is better positioned to know these loose things: "So, Mr. Johnny, never mind pens and magazines. What in your opinion is the best shampoo on the market for the late-20s male?"

From the hip-leaning Village Voice: "Don't you find it ironic that you're achieving fame as an underground hand-drawn magazine writer, when the raw material is sitting right under your nose every day?"

After which I stroked my imaginary goatee, grabbed and waved a stick pen, and gave a knowing answer: "The public lacks an appreciation for this common everyday item. Crossword puzzle writers don't bother to use the correct name for pen components. It's the 'tip,' for example, not the 'nub.' And you have no idea how much testing goes into the industrial design phase. Until the Marketing Department 'takes it away.' Now the Japanese, they make a fine roller-ball pen."

The Man Who Knew the Answer, Part 1

I want to thank all of you who participated in the naming contest; I have the pleasure of announcing the winning entry. Reflecting his sartorial symmetry and comfort in his surroundings, and obedient yet well-adapted kids, I have concluded he merits the name: "The Man Who Knew the Answer." Moreover, in recognition of the respect he has generated, I decided to present to his children custom-made pens I invented, so designed that they change color through time. For those who work here, ink is ink. That inks of different colors can sit in a reservoir without mixing or dropping at similar speeds is likewise no surprise. But to two young kids, to watch a pen change color at random without pressing a button is somewhat magical. And therefore to see the children of The Man Who Knew the Answer display such excitement and express such gratitude is beyond words.

The only way I can thank them for appreciating my small effort is by withdrawing the Shakespearean Burn that was planned for this month. I think I'll leave it at that.

A Posse for Johnny

As an experiment, Johnny joined the waiting list at the Queenstown Mall. Down-payment in hand, he didn't mind throwing away twenty bucks for the experience. Chino, still champion, didn't mind battling against a true outsider once in awhile—for easy money. Team Johnny had the parkas and ski hats, but not the attitude. He didn't have distorted boom box music either, merely computer generated synthesizer sounds from loud-enough but unmanly computer speakers.

Thus, when he rapped that Tuesday,

"I take the BMT into the battle zone,
You can listen to me or txt on your phone,
I can't hear you moaning, I don't have no scope,
You're not listening, you're jest smoking dope.
Chino you're known as the man of mixed race,
To the Moxie you're just another pretty face.
Your wit is quick of that there's no doubt,
But without your 'tude you'd be striking out
Unless you want to stay inside your fantasy,
Take the BMT and follow me;"

his posse—friends and loose acquaintances assembled by word of mouth—was dazed that he could combine such words, though Chino's thumbs-downed it because his technique fell outside the regulation format. Like I said before, Johnny expected to lose, but as he explained to Happy Hair on the way out, while both were walking rapidly, "The crowd chooses the winner by acclamation. Each battler has his own crew, yet in total there's no bias. How does that work? Is it because they've paid? Or is it that's the type of spectator a battle attracts?"

Happy Hair, meanwhile, was aghast that Johnny was, unknown to him, an expert at synthesizer mixing, a sentiment which Mano quickly seconded. "That's what happens when you have an engineering professor who builds acoustic speakers in his garage," Johnny explained.

"OK then," Happy Hair persisted. "The Moxie?"

"Uh," Johnny blushed. "That would be me, I guess." Johnny sensed disappointment at his failed trial balloon.

The triumvirate was anxious to celebrate, but being anxious also to bar no holds, they held fire until Saturday, when they proceeded to AKH#4, their neighborhood bellwether.

An unexpectedly diverse crowd rolled in that night. Johnny was unexpectedly riled as he stood at the bar for the first round and was accosted by too much "fatting out," that is, patrons occupying more real estate than necessary to lessen competition for the bartender's attention. The evening was starting on the wrong foot, Johnny dreaded. When he reached pole position, a late-40s British woman with mutton-dressed-as-mutton style tapped his shoulder from behind.

"Why, this is Manhattan! I'd have thought they'd have more bartenders?" she wondered.

"The co-pilots are in the back," he replied. "They should be right out."

"Is it rather a long wait?" she asked.

"It has been," he replied glumly.

She extended a half-limp hand. "Mrs. Stephanie Freelander. Pleased."

He accepted the hand and assuaged, "My name's Johnny. It shouldn't be much longer. I'm second or third, and then you'll be..."

At that moment, though, a gap appeared to his right, which she quickly darted into and shouted at the bartender, "Two pints of lager and a gin-tonic, luv."

Johnny was mildly shocked. There goes the British stereotype, he thought.

"Sorry," she said, after seeing him gape. "I had to *jump* right in there."

"Don't worry," Johnny responded a moment later. "I'll get my revenge."

Johnny mumbled to himself en route to the standing room table, still a little incredulous. "She's a freeloader all right."

"Happy Hair," he grumbled after setting three beers on the table, "you told me the British love to wait in lines. An old English biddie blatantly cut in front of me when I was ordering."

"Must have been a Bolshie Brit," he answered. "Did she have a coarse accent?"

"Yeah, kind of," he said upon contemplation.

"Masterpiece Theater is the exception that proves the rule, to be honest. Maybe this is a good omen," Happy Hair reasoned. "Like they say in Jersey. 'I just stepped in *shit*,' they say."

Johnny shrugged. He wasn't happy, Jersey-guy jokes or no Jersey-guy jokes.

A while later, Mano was at the bar buying his round and Happy Hair was in the men's room. Two young women approached the table, looking flustered at finding no empty space in the now-crowded bar.

"Do you mind if we share your table?" one asked. She had long, light brown hair. Her companion's was dark brown.

"I'm not doing the windmill here," he responded, to blank faces. He mentally palm-butted himself. Why would these two young women know this particular inside joke? "I'm not double fisted," he clarified. More blank stares. "I'm not drinking all these myself," he clarified again. "You're welcome to stay if you don't mind thinking thin."

The spokeswoman had a slight accent, which Johnny had trouble placing. They didn't act like locals, yet seemed too comfortable in the environment to be tourists. He wasn't pleased they had invited themselves. Still, asking to share a table is a lesser offense than cutting in line at the bar. Moreover, it was Mano's and Happy Hair's space they were occupying, not his. In any case, Mano and Happy Hair were taking their sweet time returning to the table, which caused a frustrated Johnny to stare at his watch repeatedly.

"Are you sure you're not drinking all this beer yourself?" the woman with the light brown hair asked, smiling and pantomime-style "windmilling" two beers simultaneously.

Johnny smiled, too. He liked her benevolent, quick wit. "If my friends don't return soon, I'm gonna." He paused and mulled for a moment. "You don't have New York accents."

"No, of course not," the light brown answered. "We're from Colombia. We're visiting relatives."

"Why is your English so good?" Johnny asked.

"All well-educated people from Bogota speak English," she laughed.

"It's the Colombians who live in Queens who speak Spanglish. My name's Ana, by the way, and this is my sister, Teresa."

"Nice to meet you both. I'm Johnny." He pondered for a moment. Ana had been getting the better of him, so he decided to toss a little sand in front of the wheels.

"Why Ana?" he asked.

"It's short for Mariana," she replied.

"Oh," he said. "I suppose Johnny is long for Juan."

By then, Happy Hair and Mano had returned, yet Johnny didn't miss a beat with Ana. The other three were quizzing each other.

Mano noticed the glasses emptying and signaled to Johnny, whose turn it was. "Gotcha, Mano." He twirled his index finger in the air, in a gesture that implicitly inquired did they want the same again. They both nodded.

"Ana, let me see if the bartender can mix one of your national drinks. What will it be? A *caipirinha?*"

"No, silly," she laughed. "That's Brazil. Guess again."

He shrugged. *"Mojito?"*

"No, that's Cuba," she countered.

Johnny shook his head.

"My favorite is *Ron feijoa,*" she concluded. "Rum with *feijoa* juice. I'm sure they will not have this here. Two glasses of red wine will do fine, please."

"Fay-hoa?" he attempted.

"Feijoa," she repeated. "It is sold by all juice vendors in my country."

Johnny was intrigued.

"There are many Colombians in Queens; a greengrocer should sell this," she continued.

"Where do you suggest I try?" he asked earnestly.

"I don't know," she explained with regret. "This is our second time here. Most of our family is in L.A. In California, the fruit can be grown fresh."

"I'll look around," Johnny promised.

"Oh, look at the time!" Ana noted. "We will have to take a rain check on the *vino*. We shouldn't leave *tia* at home too long."

"Tia is your other sister?" Johnny asked innocently.

"No," she laughed. *"Tia* means 'aunt' in Spanish."

Johnny sighed again. She tapped him on the shoulder to make him feel better.

"Do you use email in New York?" she asked.

He smiled, when, after about five seconds, he realized this was light sarcasm and she was asking for his email address. He pulled a crumpled business card out of his wallet and handed it to her. She stared at it for a few moments.

"You make pens?" she asked.

"They don't grow on trees," he explained. He then looked expectantly at her.

"Oh, yes," she said, and took a clean card from her purse. It was his turn to stare. "You're going to have to explain," he admitted.

"I work for my father's real estate company in Bogota. We rent houses to embassies," she told him. "You will write to me?"

"Sure, why not?" he pledged. "You will write back?"

"Si, claro. Yes, yes!" she agreed in return. "We must go now. Let's go, Teresa."

She motioned to Teresa and smiled at the triumvirate. She said *besos* and Teresa mouthed the same word as they squeezed out of the yet-more-crowded bar.

Happy Hair and Mano were relieved to have their table-for-three back, though Johnny remained in a zone.

They paid no attention to the connection Johnny made with Mariana, and didn't conceive of any reason he'd be in a world of his own the rest of the evening.

On the way out, Happy Hair was discussing a subject that normally would excite Johnny a great deal, a profound non-sequitur, walking again at great speed.

"How," Happy Hair wondered, "does the hero of a great novel *noire* correctly know when it's time to get out of town and leaves without telling anyone, without anyplace to go? When he puts the stick into drive and declares 'time to blow this clambake,' where does he *go?*"

"To a clambake works for me," Mano stated.

They continued walking, Happy Hair back to the apartment and Mano to Happy Hair's couch, *aka* his second home, Johnny all the way to the *feijoa* orchard.

Johnny took Ana at her word, as he remembered, that she promised to write first. This was not the way it happened, but even so, Johnny convinced himself that she would read his message but not return it. Still, dictionary in hand, he felt it necessary to craft a precise note. A serious, but casual, note.

"*Que tal,*" he wrote, and then erased. "*Mariana,*" he wrote, and then erased. "Screw it!" he said in a whisper.

Ana,
I bought a feijoa from a market in Woodside, but I must have written the name down wrong. It was close to inedible. My roommate, Happy Hair, who you met, told me to mash it like an avocado, and I persisted, to my dismay.
How was your trip back? Do you and Teresa miss your Tia?
Adios,
Johnny

If she was going to write back to anything, this was it, he concluded.

Don Estimado Johnny, (she wrote teasingly)
You silly man, you are supposed to drink the feijoa juice, not eat the fruit. Go back to Woodside and try again.
When do you visit Bogota?
Abraças,
Ana

He wrote back immediately.

Dear Ana,
As soon as I learn enough Spanish to get by.
AFF,
Johnny

Johnny,
AFF?
Ana

Ana,
A Faithful Friend.
Johnny

Johnny,
You are so sweet.
I look forward to showing you my city.
Ana

Ana,
Me too.
Johnny

Johnny,
I already know where I'm taking you. 'When the beat brings a beer,
it's hard to get parted.'
Ana

Ana,
I like that. Is it a Colombian saying?
Johnny

Johnny,
No, it's by an American woman named Lisa Buell.
Ana

Ana,
It's cute, and not too sweet. May I use it?
Johnny

Johnny,
Of course you may; it doesn't belong to me. Johnny, I'm curious. Your
part of New York is very Italian Catholic. Do you have the tradition
of religious festivals like we do in Colombia?
Ana

Ana,

We most certainly do. Do you have the concept of "Hung up on a
Dream" there?
Johnny

They both blushed—she because his question was surprisingly,
though expressively, forward; he because this was a random question,
and he let slip one of his influences. He was no Shakespeare after all.
Though Ana wanted to inquire about the poem, or song, she had second
thoughts.

Johnny,
OK, I better go rent some embassies. Write back tomorrow.
Besos,
Ana

Ana,
OK. Till tomorrow,
Johnny

The Groupie and the Damage Done

One morning the next week, Johnny received a seemingly innocent email from Chloe in the Purchasing Department. He should have realized though, that an unprompted email from a near-stranger can be more than innocuous. Chloe wrote that her boss wanted a second opinion about suppliers, and because of Johnny's experience in product testing, perhaps he had a suggestion. Being overqualified, she knew the answer already, but that was not the point. The point was this was fan email, not ordinary email.

We needn't bother guessing whether Johnny drew this conclusion, because she quickly made her interest known. Chloe did not feel the need to get to know him, because she and her friends had already checked him out: they were among his possé at the rap battle. Though she didn't have the wit of Mariana or the magnetism of Rachel, she was attractive, kind and always there for him. He'd never worry about whether he was catching her off-guard, for example. In her own way, she didn't mind Johnny interrupting her. "Oh, sorry, gotta do this first," we could imagine her proudly saying to anyone but.

When she needed a "second opinion" for her overbearing and under-qualified boss, Mr. Bobardi, Johnny was pleased to oblige. Mostly he didn't take her for granted, and mostly he didn't take advantage. He did not sense a soul mate relationship, though, actual or budding.

It would prove complex for Johnny to risk manage these three. Though he adored Rachel, he downplayed the possibility, considering her half-woman, half-muse, half-too-self-restrained. Meanwhile, Johnny and Ana were becoming great pen pals. When his email inbox highlighted a new message, he would brighten but simultaneously wonder why a multilingual world traveler would continue to write, even more so as he could not see himself showing commitment by hopping a plane to Colombia. Where would he stay? How would he communicate with people? What would his parents say? What is there to do in Bogota aside from hang out at *feijoa* stands?

Around this time, Johnny's boss, Harry Benton, called him into his office. As they hadn't had an industry discussion in several weeks, Johnny was apprehensive. When he found out the topic was the multicolored pens he wrote about in Issue #11, he became more apprehensive. Was this activity permitted for a non-R&D employee? If so, should Johnny have informed his boss before publishing it in *The Pengineer*? After all, there might be patent opportunity issues involved. And then there was "the secret."

Johnny's paranoia was unnecessary. Mr. Benton copiously absolved Johnny for neglect, though factually Johnny was apologizing in advance for "the secret," which remained so. Indeed, senior bosses were interested in introducing the multi-color pens as a product line, and naming Johnny senior project engineer. The cost of losing patent time advantage they downplayed, as industrial espionage revealed that competitors had no design plans for anything similar, and in any case expected costs were well below benefits. Moreover, without Johnny's heart-warming story about the Man Who Knew the Answer family, the bosses would not have recognized the serious potential for the pre-teen market.

Though Johnny was not formally asked whether he wanted to proceed, there wasn't really a choice. People only turn down generous promotions in romantic comedies and change-of-pace sitcom episodes. Perhaps more ironically, and indicative of his respect for Johnny, Mr. Benton asked for no more than a prototype before pushing ahead. It would be flattering for anyone under the age of 30 to be appointed project leader, and Johnny was duly flattered. He knew, though, that this was just a slightly creative idea from an ordinary engineer, and the more qualified technicians would resent his promotion.

This proved, nonetheless, a point of inflection. For the first time, his personal and professional lives were accelerating. His restlessness diminished, as he newly grew into his routine, consisting of emails from Ana, visits from Chloe, incidental daydreams about Rachel, ideas for the slam book and weekend carousing with Mano and Happy Hair, to say nothing of a fulfilling job designing and testing prototypes.

An Omen of his Own

A few weeks later, he became aware of someone else from Happy Hair's college in the habit of hanging around Rachel. This was Kerwin the Preppie. Johnny didn't mind in principle that another man had affections for her—something would be wrong with this world if many didn't notice her charm, all's fair in love, war and fatting out at the bar—but it would be sickening if she fell for this smug someone else. He wore the uniform of a preppie, which gave him the semblance of a robot, and he was too overconfident for his own cause. He accepted that Happy Hair was on good terms, but those two had plenty in common—the same freshman and sophomore year academic requirements, compulsory tailgating before the football team's mandatory Saturday afternoon calamities, defending a very embarrassing school mascot, etc., but if Happy Hair had shaved more often...no, I'm not contemplating that direction.

On Johnny's mind was how to protect his sphere of influence—the stress was causing his shortness of breath to return—but the answer was he was powerless. Johnny had too many ideas and events in his head to consider whether and if so, how to discuss this topic with Rachel, leaving the matter to take its own course, the downside being that Johnny could not establish if the Preppie was a true rival.

It is a fine line, naturally, between keeping one's distance and being impolitely anti-social. If Johnny thought about the potential for the Preppie to influence Rachel's opinion, he might have blocked the communication line by feigning sincerity and opening empty conversations about topical events or the college football team, so steeped in this as he was from Happy Hair's obsession. In fact, Johnny cared nothing for the Preppie's views or well-being, but considered him a threat, which made matters worse. To be honest, though, the Preppie didn't look the type who would try to steal an acquaintance's girlfriend.

He felt he could not mention his anxiety to Happy Hair.

"Mano," he said silently at his cubicle. "Can I tell Mano?"

"I'm so angry," Johnny then said at normal volume. "Can I tell Mano about my dilemma? No, I can't tell Mano. The thing is, he represents the worst in a person I can imagine, a snobbish, tweed-wearing...So his father's a partner at Wolfram, Greyslaps & Co. So he's got a *car*. He's ripe for parody! I don't want it to be obvious. I'll concoct a diametrically-opposite character. A self-righteous, politically correct, all-black-wearing..."

He paused about ten seconds before reverting to internal monologue. "I don't want to skewer him, merely for him to go away. I'm not writing this. He wins this round."

"No, Johnny," Jen said. "You can't do that. This isn't your bully pulpit."

"Oh, sorry, Jen," he apologized. "I didn't realize you were listening."

Jen was the girl from the cubicle next door. She, like Johnny in his first five years with the company, was a nine-to-fiver with no exceptional responsibilities. She was the type who applied herself reasonably in the office, but had no trouble switching off after the day was done. She *looked* and *dressed* as you would expect a late-20's female mechanical engineer from a second-tier upstate New York school, though—trust me on this one—it is not possible to stereotype such a *personality*.

Though Johnny normally kept his guard up, reflecting his principles against gossiping, he spilled every bias against the Preppie.

"What's his last name?" she asked.

Johnny paused. A gallows laugh followed. "I dunno. I only know his nickname." He laughed again. "Maybe he doesn't consider it derogatory."

His frustration with the Preppie disappeared and he became engrossed with Jen. It was not a real dialogue, but rather Johnny opening up and establishing his dependency on her.

That night, he awoke startled from a dream featuring Jen, the first time he had given her consideration, conscious or semi-conscious, outside the office. In this reverie, she was too muscle-bound for the clothes she normally wore, but no less opinionated. However, the opinions were expressed through piercing, desire-filled eyes, as she straddled him, staring down. She had memorized all his poems and was lip-syncing her favorites. She had been for months the receptacle of his off-hand ruminations, those which were preferably information kept to herself, until this dream. She had kept them to herself, until this dream.

He awoke suddenly, startled, realizing she knew his secrets. The next morning, would he see her in the shapeless clothes she normally wore, or would he see in her the smoking-hot pugilist she was in his vision?

He arrived at his desk earlier than normal, to observe Jen's arrival and decide whether to view her in the new light, or whether this was a crazy dream. There was something compelling about a strong and confident young woman capable of speaking desire through her eyes, as well as keeping secrets—his and hers. If her uptight manner could be explained by the repression of feelings, then presumably this would disappear once the feelings were out in the open. And with attributes such as those above, it didn't matter what she looked like on the outside.

On the other hand, were this symbolic, or meaningless, he would need to erase its disruptions as quickly as possible. Introducing the subject would be a non-starter—even a breezy "you were in a dream I had last night"—because she was capable of jumping to conclusions without delay. And if "uptight" was her defining characteristic, the implications did not bear thinking about. These two shared conversations and exterior monologues for close to three years. It was only dawning how well they knew each other, and the potential for jealousy at his progressions in recent months. They joined the company during the same college recruitment drive, and their advancement levels had been moving in lockstep. Conceivably, she felt partially responsible for and deserving of his success.

When Jen arrived that morning, Johnny followed her out of the corner of his eye—for presentation's sake seemingly buried in calculations—but practicing to himself return desirous stares and the phrase "we should finish what we started last night." But he didn't notice anything new or different. After about five minutes, he raised his head abruptly and stated, "Jen, when did you get in? I must have been engrossed in this study..."

"Writing another poem?" she asked.

"No," he replied. "I was speccing the test for a new pen. In any event, I spend enough time working at home. I designed the changeable ink pen in my bedroom. This is a reasonable tradeoff." What an idiotic and defensive reply, he concluded. He relaxed and paused. "How was your commute this morning?"

"The same cowboys whiplashing us on the train as normal," she replied huffily. "How was yours?"

"I woke up earlier than normal for some reason. I couldn't get back to sleep after a nightmare...I missed The Man Who Knew the Answer on the bus..."

"Return to tacky town," she stated, randomly and indifferently, and turned her head away.

Jen was, indeed, no different, no less opinionated. Significantly, though he hadn't been working on a study, she did not detect he was eavesdropping.

"Perhaps I've been over-interpreting this," Johnny mouthed silently. He pondered. "A sure case for future study, though."

The Burger Cottage, aka The Night of the Scorpion Bowls

Johnny was becoming more attracted to Rachel and, if asked, might truly have admitted it. However, this attraction was not yet the kind that would cause distraction. If so, he certainly would have radiated, then or since, at the notion of her praising his practice poem. Rachel, for her part, recognized the magnetism more immediately, but was not interested in chasing a sparkless star.

However, when he saw her on the floorboards at the Burger Cottage, he seized the notion that the emotions she displayed through dance were identical to those he revealed through poetry. Uninhibited and compelling. Mesmerizing. He absorbed her expressionism as if it was an exclusive museum exhibit from the grandmaster. Just as his poetry was unrelated to the frame of a mechanical engineer, so her unconventional, exploratory dance steps were unrelated to the brain of a consumer marketing specialist. The band shell girls couldn't temp for Rachel's secretary.

Though this was to prove a most incredible night of his life, he was not able to connect the dots quickly enough.

A while later, Happy Hair and Johnny were leaning against a wall, in a manner that suggested the wall was necessary for support. It had been a long day for both. Over walked Chloe, in a happy-friendly mood, still wearing her coat.

"Thanks for inviting me, Happy Hair," she said. "What's the occasion?"

"Mano wanted to celebrate five years of living in New York without getting mugged," he replied.

"So, in other words, because it's Friday?" she guessed, in a way that implied Mano was abbreviated from "man overboard," as opposed to *"mano a mano."*

"Yeah," Happy Hair admitted aloofly. "Any excuse to party."

"I'm glad he selected The Burger Cottage," she continued. "Me and my friends used to come here on breaks from college. The burgers are awesome."

"Mano chose it because he likes the waiters," Johnny noted. "He has a favorite who, after taking a table's order, reminds them, 'and remember, Tipping is not a city in China.'"

Chloe and Happy Hair giggled.

"And don't forget there's the Scorpion Bowls," Happy Hair added.

Johnny continued, "One time we were here, Mano got into the act, poorly I might add. He replied to the waiter, 'Do you mind that I only have chump change?' The waiter rolled his eyes and said, 'Is okay. We're not proud.'"

This Mano decided was knee-slappingly funny. Johnny relived the knee-slapping moment and smiled internally. "Mano was overwhelmed," he concluded. "Well, you know Mano."

"Overboard, overwhelmed, what's the difference?" Chloe volunteered.

Johnny frowned. He didn't like the idea of Chloe supplying a fitting punch line while his emotional mind was engaged, and who was she to belittle Mano? "He's got a life jacket," he countered, as neutrally as possible.

She pulled a small wrapped package from her pocketbook and handed it to Johnny. At this moment, both he and Happy Hair straightened up and away from the wall.

"So the wall is capable of holding itself up...," Chloe said wryly.

Johnny opened the package to find an expensive pen. Both he and Happy Hair were speechless; Johnny adopting a visage of bewilderment and Happy Hair one of surprised satisfaction. Chloe wore an aspect of anticipation.

"I don't know what to say, Chloe. It's really nice," he replied, and blew her a kiss.

She spoke with pride. "Happy five years of Mano not getting mugged in New York! A man of your stature should not be writing *The Pengineer* with a stick pen."

He leaned over and gave her an affectionate hug. Happy Hair smiled smugly and whistled: "Can't do a little if you can't do enough!"

After a moment, Chloe backed away and noted, for reasons unknown at the time, "This place is really filling up. It must be time to sit down soon."

"Yeah," Johnny agreed. "I should check with Mano."

"Let the Scorpion Bowls begin!" Happy Hair proclaimed.

However, when it came time to sit, Johnny grabbed a seemingly prearranged seat next to Rachel, rather than look for two empty seats with Chloe. She took notice, though Happy Hair did not.

"Where've you been?" Rachel asked and nodded down toward a half-empty Scorpion Bowl. "You better get yourself a straw. Your work buddies here think this is Beat the Clock!"

"Nah," he fibbed. "I'm here for the burgers."

It was a couple hours later when the fan stopped rotating. A cocktail of Chloe's frustration, Johnny's indifference, and the aforementioned Scorpion Bowls combined to bring out the scorn in Chloe, a feature Johnny had not seen before.

Thus, when she ranted about sensibilities, "I bought you that nice pen, just for you, and still you're sitting anywhere instead of next to me! Why must you take advantage of me?!?" he was close to speechless.

Johnny mumbled "Ishihara's Law" a few times under his breath, apologized earnestly, and then watched as Chloe continued to fume.

The distinction was that Johnny *took her for granted*, rather than *took advantage*. He'd survive perfectly well in the future writing **The Pengineer** with cheap, plastic stick pens, but would also be inclined to expect her attention and generosity without returning the favor. She initiated and fostered the relationship. He had no way of knowing she heeded being taken for granted. For all he knew, it powered her satisfaction.

"Is nothing good enough for you?" he asked in a tone less soft as she walked away. "I can do without the whining!"

"What the fuck was that?" Rachel asked.

"You could call her the original **Pengineer** groupie," Johnny said.

"Oh," Rachel replied, baffled.

"We got ourselves a BOND MARKET RALLY!" Mano exclaimed.

"Huh?!" Johnny asked.

"I dunno," Mano responded. "I read the headline over someone's shoulder on the train this morning. It sounded good..."

Johnny grunted uncomfortably as Mano shot Johnny a muse which read, "I love a good scandal!"

We're going to truncate the evening's reportage on that note, because that's the end of what most of them remembered.

Mano ended up on the couch at Johnny and Happy Hair's, which

Johnny did not notice until he woke up at 11:30 AM and stumbled-crawled into the living room. He'd spent half the previous night at Rachel's and the rest at home, and when he crept in, an apartment census was the last thing on his mind. He, like everyone else, could still taste the sweet, tart, alcoholic combination of Scorpion Bowls at the Cottage. Johnny, though, felt mentally content.

"How ya feelin' Mano?" Johnny asked.

"Three yards and a cloud of dust, Johnny," he feigned. Nonetheless, he was lying on his back, hands behind his head, grinning.

"Hope I wasn't too rude to Chloe," Johnny offered.

"All ill-spoken words can be exonerated by Scorpion Bowls," Mano reasoned.

"I snapped and I didn't mean it," Johnny countered. "And she'll get over it." Internally, he recalled that the ill-spoken words were over before the Scorpion Bowls had started to affect his reasoning.

"Never mind," Johnny told himself, whispering. "This is my time."

"What?" Mano said.

"I said take a shower. We're going to AKH#4 for hair of the dog."

"Before I get around to that," Mano posed, while stroking his chin like a tenured history professor, "What's Ishihara's Law?"

Johnny shook his head mentally, paused and blew an imaginary breath. "It means unprompted generosity must be performed for the giver's own satisfaction," he explained. "The recipient should be polite in response, if the gift is appropriate, but he has no moral responsibility to return the charity in the same magnitude, let alone at all. If the recipient does not express sufficient appreciation, well, tough!" Johnny paused and pondered again. He'd never have applied Ishihara's Law drunk.

"Such wisdom from a Pentel engineer?" Mano asked, trying to sound like Christian Slater in "Heathers."

"No," Johnny replied. "Ishihara's a comic book artist." He hesitated. "How should I know? Now get in the shower!"

"Yes, mommie," Mano replied. A sour look then came over Mano's face. He realized he was no longer in the eye of the storm, the storm being his hangover. "Maybe Chloe was showing 'Use it or Lose it,'" he suggested.

"Huh?" Johnny asked.

"Maybe she felt she needed to show she's capable of gaining the upper hand," Mano clarified.

"No," Johnny rebutted. "Chloe is an angel. I won't believe she's the type to play games. *I* snapped. It's that simple."

"Sorry," Mano rebuffed, "virtue is its own virtue. The empress has no clothes."

"What is that, Homer?" Johnny asked derisively. (What Mano said was more vulgar; I opted to censor it. Johnny also failed to notice that Happy Hair was increasingly cheering for Chloe, and Mano against.)

Mano was excellent with facial expression, having skin seemingly built out of Play-Doh. The effect of Mano making faces while badly hung-over was slightly hallucinatory: an insurance broker with a perpetual smile, a child with a scowl of protest. Johnny stared transfixed for a minute, after which he shook himself back to normal.

"Oh, Johnny, throw me a bone would you?" Mano pleaded.

"Now what?" Johnny asked.

Mano's face became decidedly more cartoonish. "That means humor me...oh, let me go back to sleep."

"Lightweight." Johnny offered.

"What?" Mano asked, before realizing what Johnny said. "Are you pissed off that I'm dropping out?"

"No, not when you're feeling sick, but if you didn't exist we'd have to create you," Johnny non-sequitured.

With a table of Bloody Marys, hash browns and fried eggs, Johnny felt strangely powerful. It was the kind of day he wished would last forever. He was a rising star at work, Rachel was his, he stood up to Chloe, and he had more stamina this morning than Mano, who seemed to have unlimited tolerance—for everything. However, never underestimate the hallucinogenic potential of the hair of the dog. Never. Furthermore, ignore the possibility that feelings of calmness or power are your own personal eyes of the storm, in which you're at your peak, at your peril. As in, now!

"If Mano had been any more battered this morning," Happy Hair started, "he would have been as incomprehensible as the Patagonians."

"Who?" Johnny replied.

"Those Columbian girls we met here," he explained, by way of pronouncing "Colombians" incorrectly.

"Careful," Johnny warned, "That's my girlfriend you're talking about..."

Happy Hair laughed heartily. Johnny smiled uncomfortably. What he didn't know was that Mariana's sister, though fluent in English, felt uncomfortable speaking her second language and therefore her conversation with Happy Hair and Mano was uneasy. With no reason to assume otherwise, they deduced Johnny's with Mariana was as frustrating. In Teresa's defense, though, imagine being ordered by Mariana to have a one-to-two conversation with this man's friends who went by the names "Happy Hair" and an incorrect Italian translation of "Man to Man," while Mariana had a one-to-one with Johnny.

Not having the energy to explain, he left matters alone. "Where's everyone else?" Johnny asked.

"No one answered the phone; all my calls rolled to answering machines," Happy Hair said. "It seemed like a good idea at the time, at two AM....I didn't call Chloe, though."

Johnny sighed. "We could probably use more sleep, too. This isn't an endurance test."

"Begorrah, Commish, I'm drunk again," Happy Hair pretend-confessed. "Take me away."

A few minutes earlier, Johnny wanted to drink Bloody Marys and talk about other people with Happy Hair all day. Now he just wanted to lie down and lose clutter from his mind. Even too much excitement can be too much of a good thing. Well, I just warned you about the power of the hair of the dog. Still, for right or wrong, Johnny felt this might prove a special bonding session with Happy Hair, but this is not the time for speculating whether his feeling was prescient.

He then began to gasp for breath, a factor he attributed to the alcohol. Happy Hair, being physically exhausted himself, welcomed Johnny's request to leave with glasses and plates half-full and topics half-discussed.

When the Going Gets Anxious...

Johnny and Happy Hair decided to rent a small off-Broadway theater for their 30th birthday party some two months hence. The stage manager ushered them into the rehearsal room where he outlined the generous rental cost, at which point only he understood this was the charge for the rehearsal room itself, not the theater.

"For a sticker shock price, man," Happy Hair started, "we want the Big Room."

A long debate followed. The manager didn't offer the theater at the outset because he didn't think they'd be able to afford it, and he didn't like the idea of starting the clock on the hassle involved.

"We don't have the same birthday, at any rate," Happy Hair continued. "So we can fit in with your schedule. What*ever* it is."

The manager's jowls sagged. "The security costs, the cleaning costs, the extra insurance, we don't have a liquor license..."

"Come on, man," Happy Hair finished. "You telling me the ordinary customers don't spill their popcorn and soda like it's Maxwell House coffee—good to the last drop? What's your price?"

A good deal of haggling between Happy Hair and the stage manager ensued, after which a deal was struck. A clearly nervous Johnny tried to interject, declaring the deal should have both a 24-hour cooling-off period and a seven-day pre-rental cancellation, but he wasn't heard. Happy Hair argued they could break even by hiring an '80s band at relatively low cost, which would raise attendance and hike the cover they'd be able to charge. However, this prompted Johnny to shriek, because what kind of '80s band do you think a man nicknamed Happy Hair would seek to hire?

The intervening two months were complicated, to say the least.

The stress of renting the theater wore on his nerves. The upfront room rental and band outlays, potential damages and connected headaches, the reputational risk of insufficient attendance, free-riders, etc. The objective he set for himself; to compose an appropriate poem to read onstage. Was it worth it? Was it all too much?

Partly under duress, he sent Chloe through internal mail a signed copy of *The Riff Raff Review*, a slam book he produced in high school, but it was returned unopened. She recognized the handwriting on the envelope. There really is no fury like that of a woman scorned, he wondered. This maxim he *could* bounce off Mano, who duly replied in told-you-so fashion. An apology and an attempt at absolution were insufficient for Chloe, because she wouldn't open her mind to them.

Happy Hair and Mano began spending more spare time with their own new girlfriends, which meant Johnny found himself for a good portion of these days with nothing to do.

And then there was Rachel. He was unsure how to explain that the Night of the Scorpion Bowls was not about conquest, not about a one-night stand, but how could he translate the marvel of a revelation into words? This was an occasion to avoid lapsing into verse, for fear of misinterpretation as well as appearances. Being unsure of how to proceed, he did, strictly speaking, nothing. It was the irony and the ecstasy: he dared not risk an explanation to her whom he coveted most, for fear of causing additional hurt.

Coming out of the Plants

Happy Hair and Mano urged Johnny to take the night off. Stop trying to impress everyone. Stop trying to experiment with words and sounds for a change. Stop trying to burn yourself out. Give it a rest. But Johnny could have none of that. The colors and interior design were tailor-made for him.

He flicked a remote control button and the theater darkened. A spotlight shone on a tall plant, from behind which Johnny emerged out of hiding. A burst of gunfire appeared amid the whirr of helicopter gunships, apparently aimed at Johnny, itself amid reverberating wind blowing through tropical trees. He elevated a hand in the shape of a pistol and pointed toward the far side of the stage. He ran behind another tall tree, a bright green spotlight shining upon it. The backlights gradually sparked and the drumbeat disappeared. He was now a tender electric guitar soloist. He gazed upward toward the blue seats in the balcony, in search of Rachel.

"You up there. Do you know who you are, and do you know what you are? Anyone can see the edge, but only those who have tasted the very

existence beyond...and who knows whether it is possible to return from whence one came? And what is the purpose of tasting the beyond if continuity with the present can not be assured?

"At this point, my mind slips into third gear, the gear of champions, and races toward the silky infinity. But this is not the infamous Murder Mile of the daybreak Sunrise Highway, and I must brake lest the glare of sunshine distract from this reality and crash the imaginary sports car at my tentative control before I reach the next exit."

He quieted, and the lights reverted to the evening position. He ran backstage to remove his makeup. The couples in the balcony returned to their idle chitchat, ignoring others around them. Johnny and Happy Hair were obliged to invite a wider swath than their normal circle of friends, which meant there was an uneven recognition of the purpose of Johnny's performance. To his friends and coworkers, poetry breakouts were a known quantity, but what would the strangers eyeing him for the first time take in? After all, rap battles and poetry slams were an acquired taste.

Johnny returned discreetly to the level part of the aisle and put his arm on Mano's shoulder. It was his way of signaling he'd undertaken a new type of risk and was glad it was over. He suppressed the nerves ahead of time, but boy was he nervous now!

However, we don't know how the newcomers reacted to the poems, because Mano soon brought Johnny and Happy Hair back on stage to receive a happy birthday sing-along from the audience. Mano carried a cake, notwithstanding this was a crumbly disaster waiting to happen, with the rationale that they were paying for a janitor the next day anyway...

Johnny was still reasonably sober at that moment.

When it came time to accept a tribute, he couldn't hold it. The power of the stage overwhelmed him. Being there again so soon, with all attention focused on him, produced a cocaine-effect high. He knew before he spoke that he was going to blow it. Then he did:

"I want to apologize on behalf of all of you for the way I've reacted to your bleating in the past several weeks."

He then froze, but the implications of his accusations were clear. Johnny was making this him against the world. If you can't join 'em, beat them, he implied.

He Took his Chance, He Paid the Price

Apologies were rejected before they were attempted. Though this was conceivably no more than another momentary snap, many felt he had become conceited. He sulked. Hardly anyone noticed. Happy Hair and Mano remained polite and his work didn't suffer, but he was now the black sheep of the pod. He still published *The Pengineer* twice a month, but with less inspiration, and his readers became less devoted.

His pursuit of Rachel was set back. Moreover, when he did call the next week, he was diverted to call waiting, revealing Vivaldi music-hold and his further embarrassment at not recognizing the symphony. His prior feeling of nonchalance had fully transitioned to unworthiness.

If he had shared his epiphany at the Burger Cottage, rather than gone for it, perhaps his mind would have been otherwise engaged and he wouldn't have pulled the Saturday Night Stunt or snapped before the birthday song. Oh, to know best when to share an epiphany. Oh, the fortune of feeling the epiphany itself.

With the passage of time, Johnny decided to mend fences with Jen; this was a safe reconciliation to attempt, in his opinion. He sent her a short email to regret being curt in weeks before. Though not entirely sincere, he felt contrite enough to apologize for disrespecting her neutralizing presence in the cubicle next door; he didn't realize how much he'd appreciated her pop wisdom. However, instead of pre-emptive rejection or give and take, the return volley held renewed scorn, as if the deadline to resume the symbiotic relationship had lapsed. In *her* opinion, it was too late to rectify fault lines in this casual friendship. Rather than Jen's caustic conduct and an appropriate response, though, Johnny was jammed by Jen's choice of language.

"Those were some of the precise words Chloe used," Johnny realized. It was as if for a moment she and Chloe were the same person. Moreover, Johnny felt chills rise up his spine in a similar manner. "How can two dissimilar people behave so identically?" he wondered.

Rachel, meanwhile, was in her apartment re-reading the letter that Johnny had written on the long bus ride home to his parents the previous weekend. *"It is night there, back where I started, as the population tucks into its nightcaps and nightgowns and heads into the holiday weekend as I 'clipse this bantam seat in the back of the bus,"* the letter began. The self-evident, darkened-bus handwriting gave Rachel the feeling of being next to him on this most traditional form of long-distance transportation.

Her feelings toward Johnny were not exactly mixed, though the two had spoken little since the evening he dropped the phone on her in a panic. She looked at his drawing of a proud bus blazing a trail to nowhere, meaning upstate, past decades of accumulation of Americana and families which grew up with it, namely brightly-colored roadside Italian steakhouses, ice cream parlors and antique shops, converted barns and transmission lines, enchantingly-named towns such as Lovedon and Fidgetville. She stared at her handbag and the emergency supply of chocolate bars protruding from it. "It is night there...," she said audibly. "Back where we started."

To compound the agony, Johnny began to understand the implications of his promotion. Until recently, he could comfortably balance his work life, social life and various hobbies, because none had been taxing. If work or his relationships became a stressful chore, how would he be able to enjoy his hobbies? Wouldn't it be better if everything, aside from the hobbies, was low responsibility and therefore easy?

He contemplated work. The new project would be more than a new responsibility. After he and Mr. Benton agreed on the outline, there would be few guidelines about how to proceed. Johnny was expected to know all this without training, including how to manage resentment from the older engineers with seniority - rather than merit-advancement expectations. Moreover, he was relocated to a new, larger cubicle in a different part of the building, away from his familiar surroundings and away from Jen. This he did not find unusual at the start, but he subsequently became unsettled by her absence, even as confrontational as she now was. This reaction he could not comprehend. It was as if a bread box had been fastened to a different part of the kitchen. "So what!" he thought, but couldn't shake the dismay.

Sleepless nights followed the onset of "what if" questions. "What if the project is not successful?" he asked Mr. Benton. Hoping for more than a verbal assurance that this bridge would be crossed, Johnny was surprised a job wouldn't be guaranteed in the event of failure, even at his original, lower position. Johnny now saw the assignment from his boss's perspective. *Glory* if it succeeded, *la di dah* if it didn't. No wonder Mr. Benton was quick to embrace it and breezy about the manner in which he proclaimed its potential. Johnny was becoming nervous, because the undertaking—in contrast with his initial excitement—was becoming just a big mess of ink.

First stop backlash, second stop resentment—the bonfire's thirst was insatiable. If Mr. Benton's motivations were ambiguous, the behavior of his older colleagues was unmistakable. Open hostility, the silent treatment, obstruction—and that was on a good day. His efforts were openly dismissed. Mr. Benton, meanwhile, was far too busy with corporate matters to help Johnny fight these battles.

Johnny would find it hard even to bribe other engineers to help arrange tests, which meant he had to rely on junior staff and science graduates from the agency. Why, he could not understand. Would he stand in the way of a good idea of another engineer? No, of course not. Just the opposite; he'd promote it in *The Pengineer*. Why, then?

Johnny was beginning to think it was all going horribly wrong. In reality, though, he didn't know what "horribly wrong" was. Moreover, he happened to live in a beautiful world in which all his closest friends, and their parents, were apolitical.

Nonetheless, several nightmares later he decided to confess "the secret."

The Pengineer: Issue #24

The Man Who Knew the Answer, Part 3

It comes time for me to deliver an ugly confession: The Man Who Knew the Answer was a cruel deception on my part. He exists, as do his true children, but I saw them on the bus only once. He was eclectically but impeccably dressed on that occasion, and his two children were neatly behaved, in the face of commuter rage all around that morning.

Nonetheless, I have no idea whether they are the model family they appeared that day, or whether this was merely a snapshot of grace.

I did invent pens that change color during use, and I routinely carried a couple in the hope I'd be able to present them to the children. Regrettably, I never saw them again. I did not delay release of this information to Mr. Benton because I wished to milk the publicity value for my Slam Book. Rather, it simply did not occur to me that the pens might have commercial potential.

I have no wish or desire to avoid responsibility for my actions, whether intentional or unintentional, significant or insignificant. In the final analysis, it is time to rear back for something extra, to defend myself from accusations from below about the above. Last time I checked, though, the cupboard was bare.

Before you read the next paragraph, put your favorite song on a loop in the background of your mind.

Two into one, no harm done. Wildfire up the mountainside.
Passion flying high on cloudspecks,
With you Ice Princess I long to ride.

Do the ends justify the means, or can we sidestep the means altogether?

The Pengineer will return...!

Johnny trained it to the Queenstown Mall after work that day, hoping to recreate the sensation of the first rap battle. As he approached the performance spot, he whispered the phrases he had practiced in his apartment in the morning.

He thought about Mariana and the growing reality, in his judgment, that he would never see her again. He spoke once he surpassed the spot.

"I thought the fires could only grow hotter, But Crazed Wolves bray because they live through dark, cold winters every night of the year, And summer anticipation exists long enough only for autumn disappointment to set in, to serve as reminders to those with deluded dreams."

This did nothing for him. Indeed, revelations do not occur when or where we need or expect them. And though there were no revelations to be absorbed that afternoon, this was the beginning of a first and important realization, specifically involving his emotional reasoning. He had no desire to engage in carnal relations with Jen; the sultry dream of several weeks back revealed she was a crutch. He longed to be swaddled by her. Not him physically, but his anxieties. He didn't want them to disappear, because he still needed the fulfillment of their source. Rather, he wanted them to be wrapped tightly where they could be controlled, and this responsibility could be entrusted to Jen. With a couple floors separating them in the plant, this was no longer possible. Johnny could resolve his own anxieties, he had that faculty, but only if he knew it was up to him.

And to think, he wrote the poem for Ana.

To see whether it would further improve his luck, he took the train to Woodside and the Colombian street vendors for a fresh *feijoa* over ice. As delicious as Ana promised, even if it wouldn't compare with the real *vendedor* version in Bogota. However, the only difference he felt was the cold in his stomach; his luck stalled where it was.

"This superstition business is not all it's cracked up to be," he reasoned.

Johnny sat down that evening with a set of prototypes and a ream of paper in the Spartan living room and began drawing and scribbling. He etched a series of figure eights and rainbows. He drafted some more. A sense of calmness came over him. "Praise be to Saint Milius!" he declared. "This does work after all." His project would not become the talking frog in the famous Warner Brothers cartoon, who zipped his lip as soon as it was in front of a Hollywood agent or an audience other than its owner. This was real. Moreover, if he could solve this easy puzzle, perhaps the impossible wouldn't be so difficult to resolve. Without notice—indeed, without Johnny noticing—his shortness of breath disappeared.

All that remained was to fine-tune the ink, in one way so the transition from one color to another could be planned by the user, in another so it would be random but attractive to the user. Even his most ardent detractors would have to be impressed with the demo. Cruel deception or not, the pens worked. He looked forward to a revenge of writing an entire edition of *The Pengineer* with his new, as yet unnamed pen. Johnny, however, began shivering. Yes, in the *warm* light of day. He was too unworldly to know what a huge mood swing was. The shivering, though, was preferable to chills up the spine.

And then reality reasserted itself again. His detractors might grudgingly respect his accomplishment, but they still disliked him and they would begrudge a proven success all the more. Relief to have surely earned Mr. Benton's long-term respect would not resolve the personal issues arising since the ill-advised speech at the theater. How would being a stressed, successful island be an improvement on where he was six months ago? His breathing became labored and he began to appreciate what "horribly wrong" truly was. He looked forward to his only solace— sleep—when he could avoid a bad dream, that is. Jen and the Preppie remained issues in the back of his mind, but so far behind the others they weren't even bad dream material.

Surprisingly, Johnny neither felt nor acted distant the following weekend, a three-day weekend, at his parents' house. He wondered whether his recent anxieties in such a familiar setting were incompatible. Though his parents would have automatically offered advice about his dilemmas—his father was also an engineering graduate from a second-tier upstate school—and they'd have done their best with the quirky predicaments, Johnny emitted no suspicion that anything was wrong. He did, however, begin to sense a mood swing late Sunday night, as he turned on the radio and listened to the ramblings of Mark Persky, *aka* Doctor Midnight.

Befitting his stage name, the man from After Midnight rambled. "To cure my internal ambiguity, I began thinking about beloved love songs, and each time I'm convinced I've heard the heart breaker, another comes long. I know the song wordperfect, but for Chrissakes the single is out of print. It was empyrean...poignant, baby. No less, this morning a bootleg tape entered the mail room. Listen for yourself." He played "The Last Time I saw Julia" by the Butterfly Confesses, twice, and then played radio silence for a good ten minutes. Johnny listened to the hush—more than he listened to the song, in fact—and began to think about how people grow up and become more responsible as they grow older. He thought about his parents, asleep, on the other side of the house. His calmness had been a product of the comfortable environment.

In high school, listening to Doctor Midnight was as routine as writing slam books. Though it had been several years since he'd heard a late night sermon from the Doc, Johnny didn't feel nostalgic, or unsettled. Rather, he was anxious to return to Queens to figure out his future. By the end of the radio silence, he was ready to go.

Pieces of Eighteen

Johnny was apprehensive, as this was his first attempt to set the scene with a prospective girlfriend. He had always, earlier, gone with the flow, did what came naturally, or failed to receive the signal and missed the opportunity altogether. She, they, could have told him so he'd learn for the next time, but that's another story, another time. Still, he felt quietly confident as he waited for Rachel at AKH#4, where he'd have home field advantage. He requested a quiet but not grand table; he didn't want to corner Rachel, didn't want her to feel on the spot. He nursed a weak cocktail as he anticipated her entrance. He had arrived early, needing liquid in his system—citrus, non-carbonated. He alerted the waiter to his role in the game plan. Rachel should have a Planter's Punch within moments of sitting down; the drink should not be there beforehand, lest it grow watery if she is delayed, or intentionally late.

She was late, as Johnny imagined the seconds dropping like grains of sand down an hourglass, but only 15 minutes, a reasonable margin of error.

She arrived looking distracted, as if having hurried from something somewhere more important, as if this was an errand. He knew it was going to be a short date. Accordingly, he opted for a quick launch.

"Rachel," he started, "I have to admit, I'm disappointed."

"That we didn't have more evenings like the last time we came here?" she suggested sarcastically.

"No, the opposite," he replied assertively. "The failure of our relationship to develop naturally, gradually. I thought that..."

"Hold on," she interrupted. "I defended you after the night at the theater, but then you called me the Ice Princess!" she wailed.

"Yeah," he stated, more confidently. "I did."

Her eyes began to shake. "You bastard!"

"What are you talking about?" he asked, now beginning to quiver, anger transmitted across the table. "Don't you know what the Ice Princess was? Don't you remember?"

"It?" she queried.

"Yes, it," he replied.

"I don't understand," she said

"Was this all a mistake?" he asked.

"Are you calling me a mistake?" she asked accusatively, puzzled about the meaning of his question.

"No." He paused. "No." He paused again. "No. No. The disconnect."

She gazed bewilderedly. "Now I'm even more confused."

"Are you coming Saturday?" he asked.

"Yes," she admitted. "I suppose."

"All will be revealed," he assured her. "I don't how know," he said under his breath, before concluding with, "but be assured, all will be revealed."

"Okay," Rachel replied, unsurely. "I think I may detect a note of sincerity in your voice."

"Let's drink up," he said. "I know you've got other things to do, and I know what needs to be done."

They finished their drinks, rose, and walked toward the door. They hugged, her eyes becoming more affectionate as she looked beyond him. He touched the crown of her head and reminded, "Until Saturday."

She smiled, fondly but apprehensively. They parted.

In turn, there were two items to address—the first the presumed insult to Rachel, the second the widespread contention that he was self-absorbed and insensitive. Everything and everyone else could take a number. He was resolved: no more mischievous behavior, no more self-motivated superfluous provocation for its own sake. He surprised and excited people before, but then lost them.

Mindful of the emotional and financial catastrophe which was Johnny and Happy Hair's 30th birthday party, the triumvirate decided to celebrate Mano's 30th in the formers' apartment, with furniture moved or relocated, and a smaller guest list. A Blank Slate party, Mano joked. Nonetheless, a full contingent of friends, rivals, Romans and Athenians was invited.

Johnny rearranged the furniture while Mano and Happy Hair shopped for booze and munchies. He also, though, re-rigged the electronics in the apartment and installed devices which were not pre-existing. The "I don't know how" was beginning to take shape, to the self-evident concealment of the other two hosts.

Midway through the evening, Johnny took the microphone from the karaoke box, grabbed attentions, and began to speak. Was it right for Johnny to steal Mano's thunder in such fashion? It was, after all, Mano's night. It was natural to expect Johnny to encourage everyone to join in wishing Mano a happy birthday, but instead—well, we knew he'd been under a lot of stress, with his interpersonal struggles and extended lack of meaningful contact with Mr. Benton. However, until that moment, not even I grasped the depths of Johnny's internal conflict, how torn he was.

"*S'il vous **plait!***" he began. He paused for effect.

"*I suppose you wonder why I asked you here on the evening of this great celebration. It is a time of great challenge, not least of all for me, as most of you know I am on the verge of a new, unknown mission. It hit me earlier this afternoon as I sat in the back of a speeding taxi cab. The dangerous spirit, that is.*
"*'Is it your birthday?' 'No,' I said, 'it's Mano's.' 'Tough then,' he said, 'I am going to make it yours and ensure that we enjoy it.' And I knew by those words that the devious spirit was speaking of his enjoyment, not mine. He laughed the knowing laugh of the dangerous gnome and withered back into the rear-view mirror. 'What now?' I asked myself, without the power to fulfill my destiny and feeling like 4:15 PM at the ski resort, when bunches of denim-clad teens prove to the chairlifts that perpetual motion is a lie, even at ten miles per hour.*
"*Do I have the energy to create another gothic horror for to live through next? And then I realized. The answer was in the back of the damn cab. Of course it was, because the answer was inside of me the whole time. In attempting to highlight, entertain and vent, I no doubt rubbed a few the wrong way. Fuck it! Get over it! Me included! What I thought was irreparably broken about the world was instead normality. I didn't need to change the world. Life is already momentous. **Live it!***"

This paragraph resonated among those who realized Johnny

discovered, and forgot, the answer, before he knew what the question was.

Johnny dropped the microphone and clutched the remote control. He played a selection of moody synthesizer music, which transitioned into mysterious rock guitar and then lively rock-swing.

He became emotional, only this time it wasn't Johnny on the verge of tears, but Rachel and Chloe, who understood immediately that his words spoke of unconditional love. They joined him on the stage simultaneously, one on each side, and they danced in place together, oblivious to all around them, colossal smiles on all three faces. There was no longer any conflict. There was no longer any competition.

By the way, you *can* sidestep the means. You can say Fuck it! and grab the ends.

In the week that Johnny was born, Hans Last's song "Happy Heart" reached its high water mark of #22 on the singles' charts:

It's my happy heart you hear
Singing loud and singing clear
And it's all because you're near.

A UKRAINIAN RAMBLE

"Brief candles burn so fine..."
Chris White

Naturally, I had no basis for forming expectations. To me, the fall of the Berlin Wall was not such a long time ago. But to these people east of the Iron Curtain, life which was not real beforehand became surreal afterhand. I was on my way to Western Ukraine to study the consequences of the Orange Revolution, borne out of a presidential election manipulated just enough to convince the electorate that the contest had been stolen. Tens of thousands of citizens were willing to demonstrate peacefully in bitter cold for 24 hours at a time, over the course of weeks, to prove the point that a free and fair election was worth freezing for.

It was also as if to shout to condescending foreign oh-wellers and couldn't-be-done-istas that they did deserve as much. The Opposition might prove corrupt and argumentative, in common with the incumbents (well, hopefully *less* corrupt), but if the outgoing president was going to hold an election, let him instruct the Central Election Commission to count only the votes actually cast. I was criticized at the time for failing to take a stand. I was not a registered voter, I replied. Touché to me.

It was a privilege to walk through the Town Square of L'viv—the regional hub of protests. My first inclination was to remind my hosts they were preaching to the converted. After all, more than 85% of Western Ukraine voted Orange. However, I gradually came to realize that unity and avoidance of complacency in source cities would send a strong signal to more heavily-contested districts.

However, my political study was also thinly-veiled cover for exploring the area known as Galicia during the Austro-Hungarian era. Often confused with the identically-named Spanish province, the two share histories far more sublime. A more telling contrast becomes evident when the phonetic Ukrainian spelling is applied: Halychnya. Much has been researched and written about Galicia, and many family pilgrimages undertaken. Family resemblances never disappear.

I've been drawn to the history of Galicia, where the seeds of great extended families remain where they started, cut off for a C-note by distance, war and communism. In other cases, traces of ancestral history have been erased by time, where time is an umbrella term encompassing Americanized names, forgotten languages, and entirely new lives, interests and careers. Perhaps the entrepreneurial spirit born in ancient Galicia would have been wasted in the 20th century remnants of the Austro-Hungarian Empire, for this spirit truly thrived in the Western Hemisphere. However, I leave families to their reunions and historians to their annals. I'm here to explore.

Formerly known as Lemberg, or "Leo's town," L'viv is the city of 850,000 which serves as capital of Western Ukraine. In many ways, L'viv is the Boston of Ukraine, reflecting size, geography, provincial cosmopolitanism, and academic prominence—too many universities, I overheard one resident lament. Both cities share a love of poets and folk idols. Unlike the modern city of Boston, though, L'viv lives for its monuments, myths and legends. I was drawn to a wishing well, where I closed my eyes, rubbed a coin, made a wish and tossed. Wishing well wishes never come true, do they? Underneath the section where I rested my arms was an inscription in Cyrillic, plus the numerical digits 41318 and one other number I could not decipher. Orange Revolution code, perhaps.

What L'viv lacks is an infrastructure. Though the Old Town is an Austro-Hungarian goldmine, where an aesthete would quickly develop whiplash, the roads, buses and public utilities have been badly neglected. Though the city's residents take pride in their Soviet-era apartments and maintain them well—they often take on a coziness that is enveloping—the lobbies and stairwells, whose pride of ownership is the municipality, would make a Los Angeles slumlord jealous. The Baroque airport terminal enjoys expansive ceiling art and marvelous chandeliers, but tragically the latter is the only item in working order.

"No se hablo ingles, or *Spanglish,* here." In this multilingual region, English is not common. Of my tour guides, only Pavlo regarded English as high up as a second language. Moreover, I could sense mental exhaustion on his part by the end of my tour, speaking a language he has little occasion to practice, and translating for local residents hanging on my every word about life in the United States. In L'viv, most people understand Polish and Russian, and can hum a few bars of German, but if I wanted directions from a person on the street, I knew to approach the youngest person in sight. If possible, that meant someone who hadn't started school when the Berlin Wall fell. It is ironic that the natural second language is Polish, and mine Spanish, because if history had intervened differently, the natural second language of many of these people might still be Spanish. But don't get me started.

Despite the history I absorbed from the Square's architecture, L'viv's population no longer resembles the melting pot it once was, with Polish, Jewish, Serbian, Armenian and other "streets." It is mainly because this city was on the edge of the Soviet Union that Ukrainian awareness remained strong. Indeed, the Communists did their best, as elsewhere, to stamp out national languages and religion. The Soviets darkened the joke by building a museum of atheism across from the Opera House.

The city's recent association with Ukrainian nationalism and symbolism is further irony, because it belonged to other countries for most of its history. L'viv, founded in 1256, rested in Poland for 450 years, in two spells, spent 150 in Austro-Hungary, and another 50 in the Soviet Union. Its nationality might never again change, but for sure, it will increasingly attract its share of visitors. This is Ukraine's gateway to Western Europe; wage costs are low, tourism excursions are affordable, and the pretty Carpathian Mountains are nearby. The airport is not one of those things, though, that I "will laugh about later."

Despite a lack of other common threads, I connected with the aura in restaurants immediately. I recognized aromas and colors of Sunday brunches prepared by grandmothers and aunts at family gatherings when I was young, in a way that cuisine in other European countries—even countries where I like the food—failed to connect. Immediately, recollections of family dogs and photo albums came to mind. And, it seems, just as middle-aged Italians really do speak the phrase *"Mamma Mia!"* Ukrainian men are never too old to have faces pinched by smiling aunts. My American friends and extended families would be advised to encounter the traditional Ukrainian three-toast dinner. As a former, world-class vodkathonist in training, I speak out of reverence.

I'd given thought to buying a camcorder for the occasion, but felt it would be too over-the-top American. In retrospect, it would have been good complement to my obsolete camera and PDA upon which I'm writing this essay. I'd planned an extended agenda: I needed to know whether life in small villages was affected by modernism as much as the cities; I'd hoped to breathe the purifying air of the Galician countryside. Alas, urgent business matters forced me to depart a few days early. Kiev was calling, but in Ukraine's capital, at the least, souvenirs of the revolution would be more plentiful.

I wish it hadn't taken me this long to visit the heartland of the Orange Revolution; the people are as welcoming as any ghost-written travel rag could promise. Of excuses, I've had a few, but I've braved visa requirements and guaranteed-airport-worker surliness and lack of common language in the past. I've learned how to ask for beer in all vital languages except one. I've been invited to religious ceremonies under circumstances that not even I can convince myself are still genuine. I've witnessed acts of generosity, bravery and tolerance that seen-it-alls in the West would skeptically debunk out of habit. But I've also discovered that we in the West hold the monopoly on urban myths.

And if sacred monuments, myths and legends are just, let my visit be a conduit of wisdom and spirit, between families and across continents and decades, after all. They deserve it.

THE RAINBOW TREE

"Thanks, bub, now it's my turn."

Bob Sherman, in *The Victory Walk*

A New Life Out There

Stan Murray dropped the last heavy box and exhaled. Though the unloading was not yet finished, symbolically this was important. You don't emit a huge sigh of relief when you place the final coffee mug into the kitchen cabinet, or plug in the hindmost of the appliances.

Stan and his family had moved an average of every three years over the previous 20, and it was—they all agreed—time to set roots. The oldest child, Jay, was especially excited; having just turned 17, he was looking forward to his senior year of high school. The family had already lived in this town, and therefore his new classmates were a known quantity. Known in a good way, that is.

He also liked the idea that his sister, Gail, would be a freshman, which meant she would forcibly have to look up to him, in his opinion for the first time. Not anticipating college Advanced Placement (AP) classes, the second semester would be a breeze, he considered. As he'd worked hard the first three years of high school, he'd be able to coast through much of the first semester, as well.

The euphoria lasted until his parents informed him of his responsibility in the new house: to clean out the attic and work shed. As a condition of the sale—the Murrays wanting a quick turnaround—they agreed the Vines could leave their lesser-used junk, and the Murrays would accept the onus of disposing it. The Vines picked and chose, but generally had little use for their items in storage.

Jay predictably dragged his feet for weeks, not envying this chore. It wasn't the assignment itself that bothered him; he didn't behave as if this task was above a high and mighty senior. Moreover, he quite relished the idea of sifting through the bicycles, baseball gloves, tools, camping equipment, and other leftovers.

Rather, it was the thought of the giant mess, not knowing where to start, that deterred him. It was the probability of very heavy, cruddy porcelain stored in flimsy, mildewed cardboard boxes; the thought of relocating and hauling this insignificant detritus to the dump in the family 4X4; the spraying, sweeping, vacuuming which would be involved. He was unsure if the electricity to these rooms was active, so would he be able to listen to whatever it was that teenagers listened to in late-August 2000, while undertaking these tasks? Having many other checklists, Mr. and Mrs. Murray acknowledged it would be overstepping matters to enforce the cleanup decree too quickly, but after school had been in session for a month, they began to lose patience.

Jay approached the job methodically, sorting through the paraphernalia which looked promising, primarily the sporting goods. He dusted, hosed, cleaned the goods, as a prelude to storing them in the corner of the garage or his closet, wherever there was room. He drafted school friends to carry boxes to the 4X4 for hauling to the dump, largely for the pleasure of heave-hoeing the boxes into the incinerator pile, plus the opportunity to select whatever junk they might find salvageable.

The general dusting, sweeping, fumigating of the rooms he bartered with Gail and their younger brother, Bobbie. Within six weeks, in early November, all that was left was a large, neat pile of clean cardboard boxes, seemingly filled with college textbooks and ordinary notebooks. The final part Jay reckoned could wait until later, given that he'd accomplished a good deal in the previous few weeks, or more than his parent's diminished expectations, and managed to gain sympathy from the rashes caused by the attic's decades of accumulation of dust mites.

His parents were glowing at the idea of finally settling down, with the belief that Mr. Murray would never have to change jobs again. Slight overachievers who are only average at office politics rarely secure long-term contracts. After busting his chops for 20 years, though, the patience and persistence paid off. Mr. Murray had negotiated a long-term contract with the Quaker Insurance Company, which provided one-stop-shop coverage to medium-sized enterprises. Its calling card was other insurance companies promised a lot, but ultimately turned out to be "one-more-stop shops." Mrs. Murray, meanwhile, was busy plotting the winter journey to Florida. With Jay going off to college the next year, this would be the last inclusive family vacation. She seemed content, as the children were growing and becoming independent, staying out of trouble, and adapting quickly to the new environment. The natural anxieties of a mother and housewife eventually eased or proved no more than healthy precautions. Sibling tensions aside, all was well in this Hudson Valley household.

That weekend, Jay scratched the surface of his final relocation chore, the stack of boxes in the middle of the attic. He looked them over without paying much attention. This was destined to be one of the last fair-weather weekends of the year, and thus it wasn't opportune to embark fully on the task. It was also time to decide whether to seek a serious girlfriend in his senior year, or whether to content himself with casual friends and search more earnestly when he arrived at college. His decision point entailed the strawberry blonde Karen, also a senior.

His mind was juggling this and a few other topics when he was approached near his locker by Charlie Starinsky—"Star" for short—the next Thursday.

"How's it goin' with Karen, Big Guy?" he asked.

"Oh, she snickered when I claimed that history class can be as subtly enlightening as a doo-wop musical," he explained.

"Huh?" he replied. "Where'd you learn to talk like that?"

Jay's literary statement, naturally, was undesigned. "Oh, uh, something I read, I suppose."

The previous evening, Jay had lifted his feet for good on the final chore. The boxes were indeed mighty heavy, but Jay knew that as the season changed, his father would become justifiably peeved if the attic was not available for winter storage.

Out of curiosity, he examined the textbooks and reckoned them to be of Mr. and Mrs. Vine's core curriculum. It would be no surprise they kept the textbooks of their major subjects and electives, and left the rest, if they were leaving in a hurry. This was a good lode for the recycling plant, Jay decided.

There were many, many notebooks, some with class names printed on the front, others with dates only. He scanned the class ones and saw voluminous notes. The discovery was bittersweet, because the notebooks were from the 1970s, and while detailed, would likely be of little practical value to future college freshmen and sophomores.

Jay pieced together that Mr. Vine had been a triple major: Eastern European languages, geology and political science. His wife had majored in modern American history. No wonder there was so much paper. And yet, from the number of pads, these were very prolific scrawlers.

The notebooks with dates, by contrast, appeared to be outlines and sample paragraphs of essays, with curious jottings in the margins. When he surveyed the volumes with a more careful eye, he saw simply a vast stack of unconnected paragraphs. These were not college notebooks.

Jay concluded that Mr. Vine had written many of the notes during office meetings: personal opinions and recollections were interspersed with business-related remarks. Though this 17-year-old was too young to gauge the significance, as long ago as the 1970s working for a bureaucracy was synonymous with sitting in conference rooms endlessly, trying to justify one's existence, avoiding the backstabber, etc. In fact, the late '70s might have been the golden age of the bureaucracy. Evidently, Mr. Vine was itching to do something productive during these years and the system held him, and presumably others, back. This frustration might have fueled other antagonisms, Jay guessed.

Jay put the textbooks and academic notebooks to one side and concentrated on the other journals, which he arranged chronologically. There were about ten years' worth, commencing in 1978. He reread the opening paragraph of the first notebook: "She snickered when I claimed that composing with a quill can be as privately intense as playing the jazz piano."

The second paragraph read as follows:

MEMO
To: All Potential Applicants
RE: This is not your brother's State Department...
Failures occur because of fraud, incompetence or market conditions. Our objective is to predict which of these will cause the Soviet Union to fail, unless it's *already* failed and we can't realize, because we believe the disinformation and refuse to undertake ground level research. We're so busy looking for minutia that we didn't see the tank coming through. According to senador-de-café-in-chief, Sunny Boy, however, that's the pot calling the pot black.

Jay gave only a little thought to these and other, similar sentences at the time, but began to incorporate them into his vocabulary. His friends took notice, reasoning at first that he'd discovered a new cult movie or TV series. Well, you know how teens are with their lexicons. Jay explained to Star, Karen, Lolo (short for Lauren), and a few others that he had uncovered stacks of textbooks, notebooks and diaries in his house while cleaning out the attic. The Vines were only going to throw them away—and hey, if he'd been able to locate useful term paper material in the piles, the salvage effort would prove worthwhile. He'd picked up Mr. Vine's language habits, he acknowledged.

His friends brushed off the new slang for a few more days until he declared during Mr. Howard's history class that, "Howie speaketh an infinite amount of waffle." Such a phrase was foreign to the English lit teacher, the ironic characters in the popular teenage angst TV shows, and so on. As his friends began to notice his involuntary new speaking patterns, he concluded perhaps there was something more to these diaries.

In fact, he spent so much time in the attic over the next week that his parents became concerned. His off-the-shelf excuse, that there could be useful college study material in the boxes—which might help him choose a major—didn't wash. Therefore, he stuck with the explanation of teenage curiosity. Though Mrs. Murray repeated her observation that the textbooks were the Vine's private material, Jay countered with the Vine's insistence that they were unwanted.

While Jay was out one evening and the younger two children had gone to bed, Mrs. Murray confronted Stan with her obvious fear. "He must think we're smoking dope if he expects us to believe..."

"Okay," her husband laughed. "I'll go check."

Though Mr. Murray was uncomfortable with the thought of Jay spending hour upon hour in the attic, he didn't think his son had turned it into a hash den. Even though the room was far removed from the main living areas of the house, and though smoke rises, he felt he'd be able to smell something. Mr. Murray found no evidence of seeds, roaches or roach clips, stale smoke, or anything else suspicious—simply tidy piles of clean cardboard boxes. He shrugged and brushed off the imaginary dust from his shirt sleeves. He descended the ladder and walked downstairs to the kitchen.

He shrugged again. "We got nothing on him. The boy's clean. And I mean clean."

While Jay was quickly fascinated by the concept of the notebooks, he gradually absorbed the substance. He was not fully ready, therefore, to share the discovery with his friends. He felt, in some way, the notebooks were meant for him. It would be a betrayal of something if he shared them too quickly.

That feeling did not last long, however. A few weeks later, he invited the crew from school, ostensibly to organize themselves for their senior year project, but in reality to read the diaries. The attic was tidy as usual, but Jay made the afternoon into more of an occasion by hoisting up a half-dozen deck, director's and bean bag chairs.

As there *was* a senior year project to contend with, Mrs. Murray accepted her son's rationale. It was not until several afternoons later, when they were no closer to a proposition, that she became suspicious again. Were the teens using her house for stoshing, boshing, or worse? In returned Mr. Murray to the picture. He could uncover no evidence, once again, because there was none. They inherently knew their son's answers were honest, because his body language was likewise non-evasive. Nonetheless, the seniors would have to identify a concrete idea forthwith, or else an increasingly anxious Mrs. Murray would lock the attic and hide the key.

It was the next session that Jay acknowledged the ultimatum, or should I say came clean about the predicament: identify an idea or face the end of the readings.

Star's concentration was elsewhere as he leaned back in his director's chair and grinned. "Ah, 'the amber whore has no underclothes.' Now, who could he have meant by that?"

The other five were startled. This was the first entry they had uncovered of a salty nature. What they had read thus far was rated no worse than PG.

Lolo had a brainwave. "As we have no other ideas, how about if we turn these diaries into a play? We really have no other ideas…"

The group meditated and deliberated. 1) There was enough material; 2) Mr. Vine didn't want the boxes, implying the material no longer belonged to him; and 3) the Murrays weren't fully aware of the content and what they didn't know couldn't hurt them. Beyond that, it wasn't a bad idea; it would be worthy of a good grade if done well—and they wouldn't have to do any real work for the senior project.

The plan was as follows: photocopy the diaries so that everyone would have a full set, each would offer suggestions for dialogue, and inclusion would be based on a majority vote. Subsequently, they would divide into two groups. The first would be responsible for sequencing the dialogue, the second for designing and constructing the set.

They agreed in unison, with the exception of Star, who was not yet focusing. "Who's gonna play Amber? Oh, sorry..."

Jay still had a slight misgiving. They should clear the proposed adaptation of Mr. Vine's writings, and this involved knocking on the gatekeeper: his mother.

She reacted predictably—sharply resistant at first, but calmer when she bore in mind this undertaking would keep them indoors, build teamwork qualities, and forcibly organize themselves. She was perturbed that the teens were secretly devouring the diaries, but this was rolled into an insistence that Jay approach Mr. Vine formally for permission.

Jay went back upstairs to deliver the good news.

"Great!" they declared in harmony.

"Who's volunteering to scribe?" Jordan asked.

"Who's volunteering their garage for dress rehearsal?" Christina asked.

After Jay's nomination as official rep was seconded, they generated an outline and plan of action with regard to Mr. Vine. Aside from consent, the crew had many questions. By a five-to-one vote, however, none of Star's would be included. They first debated the meaning of his voluminous commentaries, and were curious to know whether their conclusions were on track. They wanted Jay to ask everything. They wanted to know everything.

They decided, therefore, that Jay should delay his conversation in the interest of reading more and drawing up a conclusive list. With luck, there would be a cooling-off period with the parents' patience. They virtually prayed that Mr. Vine would be understanding.

To allow time for photocopying, reading and note-taking, the teens scheduled the first working session two Saturday afternoons later, in the attic of course. The boxes had been pushed into a corner to maximize maneuvering space, to act out scenes, or in case someone wanted to walk around while making a point. Jay, naturally, got to study from the originals.

Act I

The teens were seated in a circle, attired in jeans and favorite T-shirts, waiting for someone to break the ice. This fell to Star.

"Batten down the hatches," he recommended. 'Tis gonna be a long one!"

"Star, I dub thee Court Jester!" Jay affirmed. "Let us begin."

"What we need to answer first," Jordan said, debating with a smile, "is did he hold on to these diaries for decades because he continued to refer to them, because he wanted a record of his life, he planned a memoir at some stage, or were they a crutch?"

"The first thing we need is a title," Christina declared. Heads nodded, Jordan's belatedly.

"Names?" Karen asked.

"*We are Pleased to Present,*" Jay suggested.

"*Fear and Loathing at the State Department; Fear and Loathing and the Iron Curtain,*" Jordan offered.

"*The Cold Warrior,*" Star advised.

"*The Rainbow Tree,*" Lolo declared.

"What's a rainbow tree?" Jay asked.

She imagined a tune and then sang a verse from memory.

"The time and place,
It's only something your mind can replace.
Imagine all that a rainbow represents,
And imagine if it grew on trees..."

"I like that," Jay said proudly.

"Yeah," the other four agreed.

"We have a title," Jordan confirmed. "This is how the play will start. The narrator will walk onto the middle of the stage." He paused to give himself time to rise and walk toward the center of the room. "He'll say 'If all the world's a stage, why are taxis so expensive?'"

"And don't say the next line until the audience stops laughing," Star added. The other five all laughed.

"Who's writing this down?" Christina asked.

"If only Gail could type," Jay lamented. "I've been dying for her to be of some use to me." He paused. "I'll take notes. We can type them up later."

Jordan found an intriguing passage:

"I called Branko in Sofia. I was angry, as I'd left three messages, but he sounded sincere when he said he hadn't received any of them. Is it part of secretarial training over there too, to not give phone messages to anyone except your direct boss? He and I had a good laugh. The pear brandy is on me the next time we meet in Vienna, he said. If only our leaders really knew what was happening behind the Iron Curtain, I conceded. The future may be uncertain, but the past is even more uncertain, he said. This was a line from a contemporary comic in his country. By necessity, their humor is very ironic."

"Montenegro…getting drunk with spies from behind enemy lines… I like it," Karen said. "Well not all of it, but…"

The other two girls signaled reluctant approval, as they had no intention of ever being secretaries.

"Ah, sweet comfort," Jay said, exhaling. Everyone looked at him. "That was one of his favorite sayings when he was in a good mood…"

Everyone returned expressions which implied "Okay, we'll try to fit in the phrase."

Christina cleared her throat:

"Today, the Deputy Secretary said in front of my boss and me, 'Viney, you're a be-it-ever-so-humble-there's-no-place-like-home kind of guy.' How is it the Deputy Secretary is witty, competent and benevolent? And accurate. Is it he's an underlying quality person, or that he's able to fly above the fog? I've gotta find a way to fly above the fog. And I've gotta reward people who have been on my side. And I've gotta find something to offer…"

Lolo and Karen looked at her and smiled. Karen proceeded:

"Snezana wrote to me today. What a grand and glorious day. I can die happy."

"And then I found this," Karen said, "um, written, um, about a year later." She quoted:

"My boss walked into my office with a young European woman. He announced, 'Vine, may I take the opportunity to introduce you to Snezana Kraljavic? She works for us in Croatia.' I replied to him, Bond-villain style, 'Yes, we've met.' She offered a humble expression that telegraphed, 'I know I didn't call in advance, but I'm here now...' Before I could react, my obviously oblivious boss gurgled and remarked, 'Small world!' I smiled, sheepishly, I'm sure. My return glance to her was embossed with: No! The world is far too big!"

Karen stopped. "And then the next six pages are blank, except for doodlings and drawings!"

Lolo, slightly weepy from this passage, picked up where Karen left off:

"A day after I received my promotion, everyone started a fight with me, even my roommate. Why am I penalized for having good things happen to me?"

The three girls loved the thread of these entries, but the boys thought it was getting a little too, well, girlie.

Jordan stood up:

"I looked up to Sunny Boy at first. Was wildly impressed by his sense of command. During a meeting at the Filipino consulate, he remarked, 'I know this area well. You see, I used to live over there,' and pointed across the courtyard. 'Same building number, slightly different street name. I used to receive your errant mail.' Sunny Boy spoke in a manner that gave indication of the street value of this mail. But then today, towards the end of a meeting, he said, 'Moscow, the money printer of last resort, will come home to roost.' What does that mean? Have I failed to notice he regularly speaks in jibberish? Then S-B spouted the phrase, 'But let us promise, this information is on a need-to-know basis only.' If I'd known that at the beginning, I could have skipped his entire meeting!"

Star then introduced at loud volume:

"Anorexia can't be a good way to lose weight. I mean, one six-pack and the diet's blown."

The boys roared with laughter, while the girls eyed each other nervously.

Star tried to change the subject in a way only he could:

"Watch out, Georgetown. The Volume Brothers Reunion Tour starts next week!"

He paused. "Who are the Volume Brothers?"
"Drinking buddies from college?" Jay guessed.
"I liked this one," Jordan interceded:

"Why is it only Gotham City has supercriminals? And where does Batman meet with his boss? Gotham City City Hall?"

"Batman must have some kind of workmen's comp, with all the heavy lifting he does..." Jay concluded.

The boys wanted slapstick, the girls preferred seductive geopolitical intrigue. Christina attempted a half-transition, in a deep, manly voice:

"Do you expect me to endorse your ridiculous plot, Mr. Blofeld? No, Mr. Bond, I expect you to die! DIE, Sunny Boy."

She looked up. "He must hate Sunny Boy, whoever he is."
Lolo completed the change of subject:

"We shouldn't question the sanctity of the Soviet Union, Sunny
Boy said. I can't believe it. Sunny Boy has gone native."

The teens assumed Sunny Boy, Timmy Boy and other foils were
composite characters. No one person could be that dopey, or that
pretentious. Still, there were only six actors. It was not possible for each
nemesis of Mr. Vine to feature.

Karen offered a solution. She smiled, "I'll be Amber if someone else
will play the combo of Sunny Boy and the other bad guys."

Star rose and pirouetted masculinely.

All laughed except Jay, who grinned uneasily. His mouth went dry
and he gulped his cola to hide his facial expression. He pointed his pen
at Star. "I dub thee...whatever you decide to call him."

After a few moments, Jordan removed his glasses and pretended he
was Mr. Vine, and Christina a confidant:

"Revenge is a very strong emotion. Everyone is invited to the
viewing gallery."

Lolo spoke up. "Revenge for what? And what did he do for a
living?"

"He worked for the State Department," Jordan answered.

"Yeah, but as what?" Lolo wondered.

"I'll put that on my list of questions," Jay offered. "While it's my
turn, watch this." Jay rose and lumbered to the center of the room. He
stabbed the airspace between Jordan and Christina repeatedly with an
index finger and shouted, "**YOU! YOU! YOU! YOU! YOU!**"

The other actors were silently impressed with the ferocity of Jay's
act.

"Who was he so angry at?" Christina asked, after a pause for effect.

"I couldn't tell," Jay disclosed. "He crossed out the name. I looked at
it through the light and I still couldn't make it out." The others exhaled.
Jay then completed the Hyde and Jekyll turn:

"Why don't they give me a nice posting, such as Brazil, where
on the beach they use coconuts for goalposts, or the American

Interests Section in Kaliningrad, where I could run riot over the place, or Zagreb, where I wouldn't mind going native. However, if I was posted to Zagreb, I would empathize with the shellfish in the Adriatic."

If the teens, or their parents, had ever seen a plate of freshly grilled Adriatic shellfish…

"Back to the questions," Lolo demanded. "Find out who Snezana was!"

"And what she looked like!" Star double-demanded.

Karen then remembered a section, which she felt obliged an immediate interpretation:

"And I thought I had problems. I offered to bring forward my round at the bar as a gesture of ingratiation, hiding my primary motivation of taking a breather from Sunny Boy's non-stop pontificating.

"And I thought I had problems. The other guy at the bar was drunk-articulate ranting at the bartender, expounding heatedly that, 'I can't take this anymore. They're gonna get me killed! If you thought ROCK BOTTOM was a place where circumstances couldn't get any worse…then CONSIDER my SECTION.' What's his Section I wondered? A covert agency? This rant was followed by, 'What would they do if instead of going to work one morning, I went to the airport? I've got ten grand in the bank. I could go to Sydney. The Aussie dollar is cheap. I could survive for a long time on that. I could change my name and do freelance work. They'd never find me. The two people in the world I care about I could send telexes now and then to let them know I'm alright. They wouldn't be able to trace the location…'

"If this employee was serious about his secret plan, why was he revealing it to total strangers? The bartender told him to calm down, and by way of illustrating there were kind people in D.C., offered the next round on the house. I then remarked,

'If you care about those two so much, why do you want to *desert* them? What *will* they do?' Mind apparently made up, his response to the bartender and me was, 'There's no benefit in taking responsibility in this world. THEY'RE GONNA FIND OUT!!!'

"This rant would have rendered even Sunny Boy speechless."

Jordan wryly observed, "He switches gears so quickly, from real, to unreal, to work related, to totally unrelated. How does he do that?" Everyone glared. "Oh. Too serious?"

"And ask if he ever saw that guy from the bar again," Christina demanded of Jay.

The teens carried on for another few hours and then called it a day. They'd finished the pizza and Cokes Mrs. Murray had generously provided, were mentally exhilarated but exhausted, and didn't want to become too involved—lest Mr. Vine exhibit misgivings.

The Three Questions

Jay, with his long reel of questions, was justifiably nervous as he steadied himself to call Mr. Vine.

"Middle Land Trading," the voice answered. It was noisy in the background. Jay had trouble hearing.

"May I speak with Mr. Vine?" Jay asked tentatively.

"You got him," the voice responded reassuringly.

"Ah, hi, this is Jay Murray," he continued. "We moved into your old house last year." Jay was taken aback that Mr. Vine answered his own phone, rather than a secretary.

"Hey, what a surprise! What can I do for you?" he asked jovially. "Are you looking for a summer internship?"

"Uh, no, it's not about that at all," he said. "It's about…your diaries. I was wondering if—"

Mr. Vine stop-stutter interrupted him. He had never considered his notes formal enough to be called diaries. "If they're in your way, throw them away or recycle—"

"No," Jay said, and hesitated. "It's not that, either. My friends and I were wondering…Can we use them for our senior project?"

It was Mr. Vine's turn to hesitate. "For, uh…" He started to inquire about the nature of the assignment, but stopped himself when he realized this was insignificant. "Sure. Up to you. Like I said at the time, we only took with us the belongings we wanted to keep."

"But the content of the diaries," Jay interrupted. "The meaning."

Mr. Vine was beginning to grasp the impact they must have had on Jay and his friends. He recalled the code he used, and paused for half a minute. He concluded that it would be indecipherable. "Where've you been, kid? The Cold War is over. We won. Not me personally, not my government, but our system. It was a long race—too long—but we won."

"Okay, then," Jay responded. "May I ask a few other questions?"

"Sure. I have a few minutes."

Jay deliberated. Where to begin? "Okay." He paused. "Why did you start with the phrase 'she snickered when…'?"

Mr. Vine responded quickly enough. "That's not the start. That was about six years later. About two thirds of the way through, more or less."

"Are you telling me that's not the beginning?" Jay was shocked. The picture of the sequence and the neat organization he had developed was shattered in an instant. "Where's the rest?"

"How should I know? I haven't touched those boxes for fifteen years..." Mr. Vine's voice trailed off. "I didn't throw anything away—that I know of."

"Okay, thanks." The conversation was proving anti-climactic. This was not the cold war idol the teens had created in the circle. "One more question. Where is WLTF on the radio dial? We couldn't find it anywhere!"

Mr. Vine laughed nostalgically. "Oh, no, it's not a radio station. It stands for 'Why Let The Facts?'—as in, 'Why Let The Facts stand in the way of a preconceived notion?' It saved time to write just the initials, as the phrase came to mind so often."

"I get it now," Jay replied unsteadily. "Thanks. Thanks for your permission," he concluded. "One more thing. I'll invite you to the performance, if you'd like. It'll be sometime in March or April."

"Sure thing, kid," Mr. Vine reassured him.

As detached as Mr. Vine sounded, it had indeed been a long race. In fact, it had ended only a few months before. If Jay had contacted him when he discovered the diaries, the answers and Mr. Vine's mood would have been much different, much tenser. In October 2000, a coalition of argumentative democrats, inspired by the determined youth group Otpor, temporarily united to overthrow the dictatorship of Slobodan Milosevic, Central Europe's last thugocracy. This was a blink-and-you'll-miss-it event to most 24-hour-news watchers, who were transfixed by the hyperbolic U.S. presidential elections.

ACT II

Despite the letdown, Jay stifled his chagrin and revealed the good news to his parents and friends. The next session was scheduled for a week from Saturday, this time in the evening. The Murrays bought the mandatory pizza and sodas; the teens brought with them a selection of junk food.

Though Jay was subdued, the others were lightning rods of excitement, and anxious to start.

Christina went first. "I loved this passage:"

"As I looked out the window, my eyes focused upon the lass on the sidewalk, image of a girl from my youth. Short blonde hair covering her face partially, and strategic freckles to enhance the visage. Gracefully slithering as if walking on air, flitting from block to block, dress flowing gently in the sunny spring breeze. I lose sight of my loved one momentarily, as the open-topped tourist bus enters into view and Plan B comes into force. Wouldn't it be great to punt the afternoon, walk onto the bus, hand the man a five-spot, ascend to the upper deck, and introduce myself to the gathered foreigners? 'Show me the sights, conductor,' as I laze away the afternoon, until dusk sets in and the freedom of the middle day hours yields to the criminal trespass known as rush hour and tempers flare like madmen. When the bus passes, my thoughts linger home to their original purpose, sense of being fixated on the primal idea.

"'Where you goin'?' Bill asked. 'I've got to go find her,' I said. I bounded out the door and off."

Christina sighed. "It makes me want to grow freckles and look for the tour bus."

Lolo straightened in her chair and drew attention to herself. "Spotlight on Lolo! I looked through the college yearbooks. Did any of you? Listen to this senior quotation: 'It's a fair wind blowing warm out of the south coast over my shoulder. Guess I'll set a course and go.'"

The other two girls were curious; the boys were starved and uninterested, not necessarily in that order. They munched on pizza.

"I missed that," Karen declared. "Was it his yearbook or hers? What kind of handwriting? Lines from a song? A poem or a book?"

"I don't know," Lolo responded. "It didn't say. I liked it. What do you think?"

"I dunno," Karen said. "It sounds like a book my English teacher assigned. Faulkner. I don't think the phrase is about sailing..."

"Yeah I know," Lolo agreed. "Very symbolic."

As they continued to parse the meaning of these words, and with a suitable lull, here's a brief description of the teens.

Jay was of average size, with medium brown hair. He was excitable, but generally well-balanced. Jordan was a little below-average in height, had a darker complexion, and wore glasses. He was the more bookish of the boys. Star, meanwhile, was tall, with reddish brown hair that was slightly curly. He was the track and cross country star, and the class clown.

Karen, the strawberry blonde, gave the appearance of admiring the straight and narrow, but would be voted Most Likely to Surprise. Lolo, chestnut brown hair, was everything you'd expect of a girl who was never happy with the way her hair behaved, and expressed mock shock about everything. Christina was everything you'd expect of a girl who was proud of her jet-black locks.

All, with the exception of Star, were slightly above average in intelligence and near Ivy League caliber. They were, with the exception of Star, a little of this, a little of that, but no overdose of anything.

Quickly swallowing a bite of pizza, Jordan offered an opinion. "I think he was definitely a spook. Listen to this section." He read:

"Welcome to the down and dirty days. The regimes are collapsing, the locals know it. You can see it in their eyes, the stifling air and water pollution and the crumbling infrastructure and productivity. Yet our intelligence community refuses to countenance such a possibility because they've grown up with a love-to-hate mentality. Their symbiotic existence depends on the survival of a monolithic 'enemy' at the expense of everything else, including, especially, reality. If I mention this, I would face retribution or be ignored. How does it feel to bang your head against the wall?

"There's an opening in another division. I know the folks. They're civilized. However, the composition of that department is subject to change, and how will I feel if the personnel manager hires miscreants and wannabe's? That part is unpredictable. What if my transfer application is rejected? How will my division's senior managers, who spend little time with workers on my level as it is, treat me, to say nothing of how Bill will treat me? That part is *very* predictable."

And this:

"'But I am not convinced,' Sunny said. 'You can't trust any old leak in this day and age,' he said. That's correct. You can't. But you shouldn't dismiss each and every one out of hand."

"I'm not convinced, either," Karen commented. "Can we Google him to find out?"

"If he was covert, there would be no record on the Internet," Jordan guessed. The teens naturally believed the Internet was an ancient invention.

"What do you think, Jay?" Christina asked. "You spoke with him last week."

A still downcast Jay responded, "He worked for the State Department. Does that make him a spy? Does it matter?"

"We're not getting an opinion out of you, are we? How was the rest of the phone call?" she asked. "What else did he say?"

"Oh, many things," he said, in an effort to divert her. "Can we get into that later?"

"Okay," she said and shrugged.

"Here's a part I really liked," Karen noted. All could tell she was almost turned on:

"'Was she talking about how small my penis was?' Timmy Boy asked me. 'No,' I responded. 'What did she tell you, then?' he asked. 'She was talking about all the phone sex you had.' 'Oh, that's a relief,' Timmy Boy said. I love to run that tape recording in front of people, especially when Timmy Boy is trying to make new friends."

Jordan continued:

"Someday, this chapter of our lives will be titled 'How the East was Won.' In the meantime, these are the three epic events of history: The Long March, The Hundred Year's War, and... Timmy Boy's attempt to get his Club Med vacation refunded, when he was 'called to Vienna on a—national emergency.-'"

The teens loved to hate Timmy Boy, but the jokes were wearing thin. Lolo found something different:

"At the departmental trip to the tavern, Carol, our secretary, whispered to me, 'I almost put my hand on your leg under the table. What would you have done?' I responded that I'd have turned to Sunny Boy and said, 'Sunny Boy, I knew you'd come around to my view. When off mike, though,' I said, 'why didn't you?' But since the chef put the entire city of Garlic, California into the spaghetti sauce, I lost concentration in all but the 100 tiny men performing somersaults in my midsection.

"I like Carol. She's the way she's supposed to be. For example, on another outing at the tavern, I confided to her, 'If I'm going to approach a pair of bitches knowing I'll be shot down, I might as well approach the biggest pair of bitches in Georgetown.' She didn't slap me. Even figuratively. She knew that I knew what Georgetown was like in the early '80s."

Star commented quickly, "I'll bet those bitches did not end up in his britches!"

"Star!" Christina scolded. "That line is NOT going to be included."
Star turned red and bashful.

Jordan spoke again. "How about this?" He read:

"Sunny Boy's at it again. I'm tapping my 'Puzzle Within a Pen' on the table and singing to myself: *I don't wanna work, I just wanna bang on the drum alllll dayyyyy*. Beam me aboard—NO, I know the rules. Whoever uses that phrase is forcibly chained to a TV in front of a 24-hour *Star Trek* marathon."

"Who can play the drums?" Jordan asked rhetorically.

"Couldn't we download drum beats?" Karen suggested. This suggestion was endorsed.

Lolo continued where Jordan left off:

"Sunny Boy rest of the autotext, etc. If it's a weekday, he'll use the word 'holistic' in this meeting. I heard a rumor that Timmy Boy's parents had signed him up for the army, to instill some discipline. No, not really, but it has literary value. 'Mr. Vine, you're sitting a little too close to Ms. Hathaway.' Okay, Carol, you're right. I'll flip you for her. 'Why are you smiling and nodding your head, Vine, are you paying attention?' Yes, Sunny Boy, I was nodding because that's an excellent idea. And I was smiling because if we implement your strategy, the Soviets will play right into our hands. 'Oh, thank you, Vine, you could be right!' To be sure, though, I could make Sunny Boy and Ellen Hathaway like each other. Then he'd have to look me in the eye. No, I can't see it. I can see him liking Florence of Arabia here, but I can't see them holding hands.

"What will happen if the Deputy Secretary is replaced and my notebooks are subpoenaed? I will be fucked, but I won't care by then. What will I say in my defense? Yes, I know the handwriting is scruffy, but it's my handwriting and I love it! No, too folksy. This is a cry for help, because there is the edge of insanity and then there is the ABYSS! No, strike that from the record, too.

"Even now, I will preemptively admit to being wrong if it will end a conversation more quickly. I've been broken, not by the USSR's endless propaganda, but by our own bureaucracy…our idea of diplomacy is to stand on the sidelines and watch all this evil happen, while accelerating an arms race in the hope that it will bankrupt the other side first.

"Sunny Boy decides to play devil's advocate. Hmmm, letting Sunny Boy play devil's advocate is like trusting the cat to return the cream to the fridge. He poses the question: should we ditch the *presidency*? Perhaps Vice President Bush has a view about whether we should ditch the *president*?

"What's more important: the truth or the reality? Answer next month. I'm gonna tease myself with the answer!

"I can't wait until the peer review of my report on the People's Province of Yawninia, I mean Slovenia, is finished. Then I can revert to pushing envelopes outside the box. Here it comes, Sunny Boy has suggestions. Go ahead, Sunny Boy, edit my report to make it wrong. Go ahead, I was recently thinking it needed deconstructivist suggestions. What? You like the report, but feel the language is 'too sporty'? Hey, I like that. Thanks, old sport. I'm still gonna buy you a gram of ear cocaine for Christmas, though."

At first so quietly attentive they could have heard a clock ticking, rowdy laughter arose as they considered the concept of "ear cocaine."
Karen then revisited a theme from a previous session she adored:

"Well Branko, well Snezana, with your riverside bistros so impossibly cozy on snowy evenings, you still permit 'fingernails on chalkboard bad' trios which are comparable to our 'cover your eyes awful' lounge singers. Oh, I wish I had a $, even a C$, for every painfully bad lounge singer I've suffered through. Well Branko, well Snezana, your countrymen and ours are not so very different. I hope no one ever reads these journals, given the current political climate. Find an American-English dictionary. Look up the word 'tired.' Every definition."

"Too late, Mr. Vine, I just read them!" Karen declared.

"Wow! What happened after that?" Star asked. "The next entry was six months later!"

"I didn't realize they had restaurants in Russia," Christina confessed, "like ours."

A Departmental Offsite Held Behind the Iron Curtain

Jay had been quiet for a while, so his ensuing show-stopper was unexpected. "How can someone so sad...be so FUCKING FUNNY?"

Everyone therefore laughed heartily.

Enough of the difficult work had been accomplished. Everyone had had a chance to speak, perform and point-counterpoint. This was as good a time as any to break the news. Jay hesitated before and after clearing his throat and divulging, "Mr. Vine works for a small chemicals and metals trading company in White Plains. The company is about five years old. He's one of the partners."

Though the teens were not aware of his other present involvements, didn't know what he'd accomplished in the past, didn't know what else he'd lived through, they were not impressed.

"That's all?" they asked collectively.

Jay concurred. They began to suffer the same letdown that Jay had experienced a week and a half before. The sad part began to win out over the fucking funny part. It was late and the mood was deteriorating. They were somber and silent for several minutes.

And then Star saved the day. He walked into the center of the room and, with his head facing down, read a passage:

"It's been a long day and therefore I'm going to take it easy on the beer tonight. I'm moving straight to vodka."

"Make mine a double," Jay said, with a tear barely visible out of the corner of one eye. He wiped it away.

They then gave each other a collective and figurative hug.

"How about this one?" Star offered, reading from his photocopies:

"Sunny Boy boasted to me that where his mother is from, the roads aren't paved. So I said 4X4s must be very popular. He said no, because they were too expensive. So I asked if they drove four-wheel drive *bicycles.*"

"What do you think?"

Jordan had a quick reply. "I think you made that up. They didn't have four-by-fours twenty years ago."

Star turned red.

Jordan continued. "We'd have voted it down even if it was true."

Christina delivered the knockout blow. "Cripes, Star, every day is a full moon for you." This was only partly true, but she'd been dying to use that phrase for hours and this was the best occasion.

Karen decided it was necessary to defend and scold Star. "He didn't mean to be sneaky...and he won't do it again." With that final comment, she frowned at him.

Lolo then read a long passage:

"Now they want me to fly to Europe to meet a so-called defector. He's going to be a no-show. I told them he's going to be a no-show. The question is: do I want a free trip to Europe. Well, Snezana is not going to be there, so I'm not sure that I do.

"Still, I railroaded through that our meetings were in Vienna, rather than Paris. I refused to endure another stopover in cliché country. The crux of a joke of our interactors there is, 'that's crap!' or 'you're crap!' Moreover, it's cranberry festival season in Vienna.

"Was he a no-show, you ask. Why did you ask this question if you already knew the answer? That wasn't the worst part, worst parts. Timmy Boy invited himself and convinced our boss it was vital he attend, and that it was my fault the contact was a no-show. No number of phone calls would convince the contact to meet us for even fifteen minutes, no amount of bribing men on the street to attend this meeting and pretend they were our contact, they had been drugged and could no longer speak English. Don't the Viennese have a sense of humor?

"The next morning in the customs line at the airport, Timmy Boy saw the line our boss was in moving faster, so he quickly left my slow-moving line and darted across. 'Do you want me to hold your carry-on luggage, sir?' My, what an earnest-sounding voice you have, Timmy Boy. Why, the better to suck up with, sir. The displaced person now in front of me observed this with 'admiration,' believing that Timmy Boy's objective was to cut in line, rather than suck up. He then shouted, 'Is that how you Austrians behave?' Rin Tin Timmy Boy had ears only for our boss. I laughed out loud, which prompted the d.p. to scowl at me. He was okay after I sighed and said, in Serbo-Croatian, 'Molim! You're lecturing to the professor.'

"In the departure lounge coffee shop, I escaped these two and sat down next to a girl with henna tattoos and much-too-cheap jewelry. Behind this covering and beneath the boho act, she was beautiful. After an improvised Mai Tai, she would return to Thailand, where she works as a hairdresser at a small beach resort near the jungle. She's a ski bum during the winter. There's my Shangri-La. I have no doubt that I wouldn't need a map."

"I think I'm in love again," Lolo concluded. "Any other comments?"

Jay did a double-take, but caught himself and began to speak before others could comment:

"I was beginning to realize that though we were treading water in the cold war, we were single-handedly keeping this jalopy of a tavern in business. Last night, at our table Ellen handed out a stock tip. For Raposa Automotive. Sunny Boy chimed in: Oh *yes yes yes yes yes.* I know the Vice Chairman very well. Raposa Automotive saw off Lee Iacocca twice. Oh yes yes yes yes yes. Oh *yes yes yes yes yes,* Sunny Boy. I know the vice chairman very well, too. Such a traditionalist he could have APed out of Divinity School. The man has a parallelogram for a head, if I remember correctly. Oh *yes yes yes yes yes.* If you know him so well, Sunny Boy, why aren't you working for him, instead of with us curb-huggers? We aren't exactly lovable rogues. We wouldn't know a four-letter word if it snuck up and bit us on the fuckin' ass!"

Jay paused and smiled.
"Who's Lee Iacola?" Star asked.
Jay continued:

"The Deputy Secretary stopped by the tavern to say hello. Sunny Boy and Timmy Boy monopolized his time. I whispered into Carol's ear: A king beats a pair of jackasses any time. Pass it on. Timmy Boy—still no pumpkin in reverse—thinks people object to his friends. That's not accurate. It's the way he meets them. My view of the manual laborer is similar to that of

Fernand Leger, with one exception. His were heroic, mine stand around all day."

"And another exception," Karen argued. "None of us know who Fernand Leger is."

Star continued this line of reasoning. "Where's the Biography Channel when we need it?"

Jay retrieved a last gasp of patience and persistence:

"Calling all heroes...where is Samantha Smith when we need her...calling all Trekkies, too...those in the latter group feel free to immolate yourselves."

They cracked up, without even knowing the definition of "immolate."

"Any Trekkies here?" Christina asked.

Silence.

It was Karen's turn:

"Washington is starting to gentrify. Developers are erecting trendy bars which are an excuse to rip off 'trendy' people— but not 'edgy' people; they're too astute to get ripped off. However, if there was ever a trade war with France and our farmers retaliated by getting Brie imports banned, the entire government apparatus would grind to a halt. The 'loud, proud and doesn't need a crowd' lobbyists would puke up their coffees! !! !!! (I get the idea! !!)"

"Okay, a little much...I have an idea. After we graduate from college and get jobs, and have some bucks, we'll have to all meet in Washington for a weekend."

There was near-unanimous assent.

"Wait!" Lolo broke in. "You're proposing that for Act II, or we should all meet?" From the looks all around, the near-unanimous answer was clear. "Me, too," she said. "I hope the next five years go by real fast."

"A Volume Bunch Reunion Tour?" Star added. "I can't wait!"

"I think we're all getting tired," Karen observed. Half the group looked at the clock. "Should we call it a day?"

But they wanted to keep going.

"In that case, I'll take a turn," Karen stated. She stood up and cleared her throat:

"I'm late for work again. I should go home and call in sick for all the stick I'll get. Why do I always end up behind the person who's never used a traffic light before? No, I must stay the course, for tonight I will 'work late' and retake the pens that have been stolen from my desk.

"It's just as well I stayed the course, because this afternoon a stockbroker called me with a 'hot tip.' I told him that on my salary I could afford four shares. He wasn't listening. He said before the initial transaction we should meet in person. I said NEvahhhh! He still wasn't listening. He said, for reasons of taxplanning, he was extra ordinarily—yes, 'extraordinarily' is two words—busy this time of year. He could not fit me in until...drumroll...tomorrow morning. At which point, I gently rested the phone on my desk, banged my head against the wall a couple times, left the building, and screamed all the way home. Some things take precedence over stealing your pens back."

She returned to her beanbag and everyone applauded.
Jordan took her place in the center of the room:

"Within 24 hours, I had calmed down. With thanks to Carol. The hotels in D.C. were full so she installed her relatives at the Holiday Inn in Baltimore. Carol, dear, Holiday Inn in Baltimore. Oxymoron watch!"

The other five teens looked at each other. "Nah...!"

Jordan kept going:

"We had a few beers after the intra-company softball game. Guess where we went? Was that me who was beaned in the head when I wasn't looking, one of the other secretaries asked? Yes, it was. How embarrassing. No? I'm a tough cookie? Yeah, I'm one tough cookie. We have a lot of bang-the-head-on-the-wall practice in our division. When I got home that night, I turned on the TV and something ridiculous called *The Garry Shandling Show* was on. Why can't those fuckheads at Channel 9 put on something more appropriate for that time of night, such as *Get Smart*. I couldn't sleep. I kept thinking about Ellen and what I said to her at the tavern. I said, 'Ellen, you may be a romanticist, but no way are you a semanticist.' I caught myself too late, apologized for the insult and said, 'You're right, I'm the triple major in this relationship.' Then I added insult to injury by saying, 'Mother of Pearl, did I just say *relationship?*' Now it's 3 AM and I changed the channel to the local CBS affiliate. Mark my words, I will intensely regret if this station ever takes the late-night movie off the air. I love the theme song. I love the theme song. I love the theme song. Good night Ellen, you can give me the evil eye in the morning."

A long paused followed, after which Christina spoke. "That's better. Not all of it, of course."

This time, it was Jordan who gestured. He wasn't quite finished:

"I still can't sleep. WLTF, WLTF, where is the Rainbow Tree when I need it? Tonight, I'm going to write to Snezana and remind her that I'm the only person outside the Balkans who can pronounce her name correctly. No I won't. That's tacky. I'm not pledging my love, but I will tell her how wonderful she is and how much she means to me. I would tell her I could not live in a country with as much air pollution as hers. She would reply that she could not live in a country with as much noise pollution as mine. Hold on, are there more like Snezana in the Balkans? Are all the girls in Shangri La as zany as Maria, *aka* M.T.? Can I be greedy? Should I? Answers: It doesn't matter, yes probably, maybe, NO!"

An affectation of peace of mind began to pervade the room, as the teens stayed silent for five minutes or more. This occasion is apt for a musical montage and a snappy flashback, but rather than suggest a selection to suit my own mood and memories, I'll leave the musical choice to your own personal tastes.

The darkness of the starless night was beginning to give way to the dawn and birdsongs of the early hours, but there was still time for one more paragraph and one more contemplation.

It was Jay's turn to read:

"It was a grand meeting. May I call you grandiose, Meeting? It was called to plan our Central European strategy and to make the peace with the politically-appointed bureaucrats from the previous administration. I paid full attention during the first hour, then drifted off to more serious priorities. After winning a few times against my 'Puzzle Within a Pen,' I began to play word association. This is what I wrote: 'I'm just a singer in a rock and roll band, there are too many people who are trying to be free, too many people who just wanna be free. I'm just a singer in a rock and roll band, I'm just a singer in a rock and roll band...'

"Enough is *ENOUGH!!!*"

That was the final entry in the diaries.

The teens paused to reflect for a few moments, and then Karen asked Jay. "Do you have Napster?"

Lolo was visibly close to tears. The other two boys inhaled.

A moment later they heard Mr. Murray ascending the stairs. "Jay, are you up there?"

He entered the room, shocked to see the teens. "What the...! Do you know what time it is?" However, when he saw the heartful expressions on their faces, he stopped. "Oh, excuse me. We'll call your parents and tell them everything is all right."

The Pact

Bringgg, bringgg, bringgggg!
Jay answered the phone. "Hello."
"Hi," Star said, "It's Star."
"Hi Star," Jay responded.
"How's the final draft coming?" Star asked.
"Nearly finished," Jay answered. "Ah, you didn't call to ask me about the script, did you? You're on the set-building team."
"No, I was wondering...I was wondering..." Star couldn't finish.
"If I mind if you asked out Karen?" Jay guessed.
"Yeah," Star admitted. "How'd you know?"
"I could see it coming," Jay claimed. "No, I don't mind. I have my eye on Snezana's daughter anyway."
Jay could sense Star coming to attention. "What? Did you Google her?"
"No," Jay answered. "Did you?"
"Stan Murray, my man!" Star said, to change the subject. "If you had not dealt your dutiful son Jay the chore of cleaning out the attic, we'd never have found those diaries!"
"Yeah, okay, whatever," Jay replied. "I think this was in our stars all along."
Star then tossed in some gossip. "Jordan claims he's going to Shangri La after graduation."
Jay laughed. "It's always the quiet ones. Anything else?"
"No, I don't think so," Star replied.
"Until Saturday afternoon then..." Jay concluded.
"Yup," Star agreed, "till then."

The Home Stretch

The teens were gathered in Jordan's garage. This was their last practice before the dress rehearsal, which was scheduled for the following weekend. Jay was the last to arrive, and when he walked in the door, he hurriedly handed out copies of the final draft. Jordan's mother brought in a tray of snacks, smiled and left, closing the door on her way out. They sat in a circle.

"Before we start," Karen began, "I want to know what everyone thinks. Did Mr. Vine get together with Snezana?"

"And did he make it to Shangri—?" Christina wondered.

"Hey!" Karen interrupted. "I decided he exaggerated about the people he worked with, to overcome his boredom. I think he really liked Sunny Boy."

"Why did he ridicule him so much?" Christina asked.

"Because he was so easy to make fun of!" Karen declared, and laughed. So did everyone else.

"Okay," Star agreed. "I believe you. But don't tell me he liked Timmy Boy!

Most everyone laughed again.

"Who remembered to sneak in the beer?" Jordan asked.

"Make mine a plum brandy," Christina replied, in the mistaken belief that this was a girlie beverage.

"I downloaded *The Rainbow Tree*," Karen cried out. "It took me about half a day to find," she continued, in a combination grumble and laugh. "It goes like this." She hummed the music and sang the most important verse:

"The time and place, it's only something your mind
can replace.
Imagine all that a rainbow represents, and imagine
if it grew on trees.
A rainbow appears as a definitive signal for all to
see, that the storm is over."

Lolo could hold her composure no longer. She began sobbing.

Jay walked over. "What is it?"

"But I want it to have a happy ending," Lolo wailed.

Jay put his hand on her shoulder. "Don't worry," he reassured her. "You haven't seen how it ends. It does."

Karen turned to Jay and asked, with some urgency, "Did you remember to download 'I'm Just a Singer?'"

Jay shot back a look which telegraphed, "Oh, shit!" Just then, Jordan's father walked in and said, "I know that song!" and he sang the opening 45 seconds or so, not far off tune. "I might have the album upstairs if you want it."

They stared. They were thankful, but Jordan's father was intruding. He apologized, before remembering why he was there. "There was a phone call." The teens' eyes registered their hopeful expectation that it was Mr. Vine. "Charlie, your track coach called. He wanted to know if you were going to be the guest of honor at this afternoon's voluntary practice."

Star shook his head vigorously, after which Jordan's father continued, "That's what I told him. I didn't think he'd be able to drag you away." He returned to the house.

A now-composed Lolo turned to Jay. "We have lots more questions for you to ask Mr. Vine."

"Yup," Jay agreed. "After rehearsal I'll write them all down. I'll call him next week."

Show Time

It was Saturday, March 24, 2001, at 1:30 PM, or half an hour before the dress rehearsal was due to start. The teens were nervous, anxious but ready. Star performed the parts of Sunny Boy and Timmy Boy, the former as a fake-mustached intellectual, the latter dressed as a socially aggressive dweeb. Jordan acted as Deputy Secretary, Bill and other part-time roles. Jay, naturally, was Mr. Vine.

Christina played Carol, who they guessed Mr. Vine had nicknamed Amber, and April. Karen was Ellen Hathaway, assorted other secretaries, and the woman who was learning how to use a traffic light for the first time. The teens took turns being the parents; continuity was attained through consistency in clothing. Lolo played Snezana and sang whatever songs were necessary. They opted against a tape deck or songs downloaded from the Internet.

They built the set mostly themselves, but convinced younger brothers and sisters to sweep and rearrange the garage, and to perform as stage hands. Gail was, surprisingly to some, a useful cog du jour. The teens chose a basic set with five scenes—Mr. Vine's office, the division's meeting room, a table at the tavern, an airplane seat, and the coffee shop in Vienna—in the view that the dialogue should be the focus of attention as much as possible. The high school drama teacher offered his considerable experience, but that truly *is* another story, another time.

The parents were there, along with the siblings, a few friends and Star's track coach, so he could see what the fuss was all about. Despite the minimalism, Jordan's family garage had been transformed. In this Hudson Valley suburb, a front lawn lined with cars indicated a gathering, but without any indication of what kind. A week later, the teens would perform the theatrical production for keeps, and then return to their real lives—the track season for Star, and the anticipation of college acceptance letters and a final summer at home for the others.

Thirty minutes later, the curtain rose, figuratively. Ninety minutes after that, the curtain fell. Although the parents witnessed none of the input, they absorbed and admired the output. That's the extent the parental reaction merits, for this day truly belonged to the teens and The Rainbow Tree Diaries.

The actors searched repeatedly out of the corner of their eyes during the dress rehearsal and formal performance, but failed to locate Mr. George, *aka* Georg, *aka* Yuriy, *aka* Gyorgy, Vine. We can second-guess his motivation and critique his decision not to attend, but we can't remove ourselves from his earlier illuminations that—despite many frustrations and irritations, regrets and would-be do-overs—the game was finished and he had won. The margin of victory did not matter. It did not matter at all.

The students would eventually disperse to distant corners of the country, but the diaries would influence them the rest of their lives. At this convenient point, I'm going to leave the teens and their day of glory. It's time for me to set a course and go.

In 1982, a ten-year-old girl named Samantha Smith wrote to Soviet leader Andropov, explaining that his feud with Ronald Reagan was senseless. She knew Americans wanted a peaceful end to the Cold War, and implicitly that citizens in his country felt the same. So touched was the Kremlin that she was invited to meet the people of the USSR to see for herself. She returned to her small hometown to a hero's welcome of banners above the town's central junction, reading WELCOME HOME SAMANTHA!

Three years later she died in a plane crash.

ABOUT *TRILOGY YEAR*

What began as a set of three inter-themed tales gradually evolved into a series of seven stories written over the course of twelve months. Please see www.atkinsbay.com for more.

Richard Segal is currently a strategist with the Argo fund management group, and resides in London, England and Phippsburg, Maine, with his wife and daughter. He is the author of *The Russian Economy* (1994) and was a contributing author to the *Handbook of International Investing*. This is his first published work of fiction. He once did work in a pen research lab, though not in Queens.